SUMMER OF NO SURRENDER

SUMMER OF NO SURRENDER

RICHARD TOWNSHEND BICKERS

Uniform Press
www.uniformpress.co.uk
an imprint of Unicorn Publishing Group
66 Charlotte Street
London W1T 4QE

www.unicornpress.org

© Uniform Press, 2015
First published 1976. This edition first published by
Uniform Press, 2015

A catalogue record for this book is available from
the British Library

ISBN 978-1-910500-28-6

Printed and bound in the UK

CONTENTS

CHAPTER I 11

CHAPTER II 19

CHAPTER III 27

CHAPTER IV 39

CHAPTER V 49

CHAPTER VI 63

CHAPTER VII 79

CHAPTER VIII 105

CHAPTER IX 117

CHAPTER X 127

CHAPTER XI 135

CHAPTER XII 145

CHAPTER XIII 167

CHAPTER XIV 181

CHAPTER XV 189

CHAPTER XVI 199

CHAPTER XVII 207

They were both bewildered when they first saw their section leaders' guns firing; flame licking back over the wings, smoke trailing behind. Then they were in the smoke slicks themselves. Something was rattling against wings and fuselage. They didn't know what was happening. Each tried to follow his leader: they were flying into ejected cartridge cases and belt clips, metal hammering on cockpit canopy and engine cowling; they thought they were under fire and flinched. They held their thumbs ready over their firing buttons, but no sooner did a bomber flash into the sights than it was gone again. Another – and it was lost in a split second also. Where had the enemy gone? Why was aiming so difficult? This wasn't like shooting at a towed target, or even like camera gun dogfighting with an instructor. A gut-pulling turn, standing on the wingtip, the blood draining from the head, eyes going dim… greying out… a sudden blackout. Recovery. An empty sky.

It had all taken less than two minutes…

PETER KNIGHT, TWENTY THOUSAND FEET ABOVE the chalk cliffs of Kent, saw his Number Two burned alive.

He had led "Yellow Section", three Hurricanes with more fire power than a whole infantry battalion in the 1914 war, into action for the fourth time that day. He and the rest of the pilots in 172 Squadron were tired and dazed after so much fighting concentrated into so short a time; many weeks of the same hard routine.

The four sections had separated, wading into an attacking force of some thirty German bombers protected by as many Messerschmitt 109 and 110 fighters. Yellow Two must have had the sun in his eyes or been concentrating too hard on firing his guns: two 109s attacked him and in six seconds his Hurricane was in flames.

Knight peeled off and dived after him, turning steeply on a wingtip to circle his friend. He saw him snatch at the rip cord and the parachute open, watched him slapping at the flames which flared from his arms and legs and were climbing up his chest as the wind of his fall fanned them. Yellow Two was dead by the time he had dropped three thousand feet. Knight jerked his attention back to saving his own skin as enemy tracer bullets came sparkling past his cockpit canopy again.

Like an incantation, an ironical R.A.F. song thrummed in his brain as he flew and fought until his ammunition ran out.

"I don't want to join the Air Force,
I don't want my bollocks shot away,
I'd rather stay in England,

In merry, merry England,
And frig and drink me bleedin' life away, Gor blimey!"

But Merry England had become the most dangerous place in the world, in 1940, and was likely to stay such for many years to come.

He had a nightmare about his friend's death that night.

The next morning he was called later than usual. The arrival of fresh squadrons from Scotland at a neighbouring airfield had eased the pressure on 172; slightly and temporarily, but an extra two hours' sleep was more welcome to the weary fighter pilots than the richest treasures in the Tower of London.

The first sound Knight heard was the Black Country whine of his batman, Aircraftman First Class Tuttle, who hated the war almost as much as he resented commissioned rank. "Toime ter git oop, sir. It's seven-ow-clock."

He sounded pleased. About the only part of his job which Tuttle relished was this excuse to lay hands on an officer: he gripped Flying Officer Knight's muscular shoulder harder than necessary and gave it a jerk.

The squadron had flown six sorties the day before. They had shot down seven German bombers for sure and claimed another two probables and four badly damaged. They had destroyed three Messerschmitt 109s and damaged three more. All this for the loss of three Hurricanes and two pilots: one dead and the other wounded but alive. So there had been something to celebrate and something to forget, as on most days. Tuttle, who was on duty in the Officers' Mess that evening, had seen all four of the pilots to whom he was personal servant stagger up to their rooms shortly before midnight, more than a little drunk.

Knight grunted, shrugged the batman's hand away and reached for the proffered cup of tea. His head throbbed and his tongue felt like a piece of thick flannel.

But it was not only his aching head and hangover which put a blight on the start of a new day and kept him lying inert long after he had first become conscious of his batman's summons. As soon as he woke he had the same ugly memory which had plagued him the previous evening and pursued him in his dreams.

All the time the squadron was drinking pints of bitter in the White Swan (known to them as the Mucky Duck) until after closing time, and then in the mess anteroom, the vision had haunted him. Even during the game of high cockalorum with which the evening had ended, he was thinking of his dead friend and the manner of his dying. In that sprawling, noisy, good-natured tangle of arms and legs, heaped bodies threshing on the carpeted floor, Peter Knight could not put away the images in his mind's eye, or shut his ears to the remembered cry. "Yellow Two... I've been hit... baling out... Oh! Christ..." And the flaming Hurricane spinning away on his starboard.

But now it was another day and he sipped the fresh, hot tea gratefully and said, by way of encouragement to a batman whom he suspected of being less than half-witted: "Bloody good cup of tea, Tuttle. Get me another, will you."

"Yessir."

"And see if you can grab me a bathroom, and turn the water on. A shower won't do anything for me this morning. I need a good long soak." He yawned and stretched, grimacing as his bruised body ached, victim of last night's horseplay and a low altitude bale-out two days previously when he had hit the ground clumsily and bruised his ribs.

"Yessir."

There was a snuffle and a scratch at the door and as Tuttle opened it on his way out a white mongrel with a black patch over its left eye and a brown splodge on its back bounded in and leaped on the bed.

" 'Morning, Moonshine." Knight ruffled his pet's wiry coat. The small dog, named on account of its dubious ancestry (the illegitimate result of some illicit nocturnal activity), sprawled on his chest and tried to lick his face.

This was also part of the morning ritual. When Tuttle brought in the tea, he let Moonshine out on what his owner called his morning recce. The batman liked the animal, which was just as well; for if he hadn't treated Moonshine with what Flying Officer Knight considered due care and attention, A/Cl Tuttle would not have received his weekly half-crown tip.

Knight lay back with his arms folded under his head, staring at the ceiling. The hammering at his temples was easing, his mouth no longer felt like the Gobi Desert Another cup of tea, five minutes in a hot tub, and he would feel fit for breakfast and the walk to dispersals; where, if Jerry would not molest them for the next couple of hours, he could sleep some more in an armchair in the crew room, or out of doors in a deck chair. He thought of the advertisement for artificial suntan stain in magazines like *Wide World* and *Strand*, claiming that "All handsome men are slightly sunburnt", which had become a catchphrase of the 'thirties. He wondered if Anne, his current girl, would endorse this. But, so far, the pilots of No. 11 Group in Fighter Command had not had much opportunity for sunbathing, this summer.

Where was that lazy blighter Tuttle?

The door opened and Birmingham's gift to R.A.F. station East Malford shuffled in with a cup and saucer in one hand and Knight's newly polished black shoes in the other. "Bath's running, sir," he announced unctuously.

Knight took his tea and Moonshine wagged his tail, hoping for a saucerful. "Better go and see it doesn't overflow."

"Yessir." Tuttle went, with mutinous thoughts: You'd think I'd nowt else ter do but run 'is bleedin' bath and fetch 'im extra cupsertea, and me with three others to look after, an' all. Roll on my bleedin' leave. Thought of leave cheered him: he had a ploy in mind which should assure that his next visit home would bring him a hero's perquisites. If the tarts was so keen on air crew, then air crew they would get. He grinned in anticipation. Norm Tuttle knew how to enjoy the perqs without having to run the risks.

He turned off the bath taps and went to fetch Knight's everyday tunic from the wardrobe to polish its brass buttons and belt buckle.

Knight heard a familiar voice singing under the shower. "Home, home on the range…"

They met at breakfast.

The bathroom baritone was over six feet tall, thin, with a humorous high-cheekboned face, weatherbeaten and loose-limbed. His accent and background suggested strange, romantic places, and he did great bedroom execution among uniformed and civilian females alike. In those days, when few people went abroad on holiday, anyone from overseas was an attraction; and Hollywood had created such a glamorous legend about America, that somebody who actually lived there could count on a delighted reception.

"Hi, Pete. Howya doin'?"

" 'Morning Six-gun. Here's a paper." Knight handed Six-gun Massey a *Daily Mirror* and retired behind his *Telegraph*. The American was a good type, but still hadn't learned that the British did not like breakfast time conversation.

Pilot Officer Burton Wilbur Massey had been a barn-storming air circus pilot who left America to join the R.A.F. as soon as Britain declared war on Germany. He could have chosen the U.S Air Corps if it were only a secure income he wanted, but they had no war to offer: the R.A.F. not only meant comfortable lodging, with regular meals and pay; it guaranteed the kind of excitement he craved. 172 Squadron set great store by his rarity: he was just what they expected a real live Yank to be like. He had acquired his nick-name from his remarkable skill with a pistol and because he wore, on duty, a massive .45 Colt at his waist, its holster strapped to his thigh with a leather thong. The fact that it was not a six-shooter was no deterrent from calling him "Six-gun". His party trick was a fast draw and he could toss an empty cocoa tin into the air and fire three shots into it while it was still overhead.

But at this hour of the morning no one was in the mood for loud noises. The day held enough of those in store. In the traditional muted atmosphere of the British breakfast table, the officers of the three fighter squadrons which comprised the East Malford Wing ate their porridge, bacon and eggs, toast and marmalade, and read the papers. The country was on short commons, but pilots' rations were generous.

Pick-up vans and 15 cwt. trucks waited outside the mess to take them to dispersals, hangars and offices. Some of them had their own cars, a few rode bicycles. Those whose squadron dispersals or other places of duty were close, sometimes walked.

Knight usually allowed time to walk, when he could, for Moonshine's convenience: there was an abundance of fascinating smells and other exciting attractions on the way, which the dog pursued and investigated with gusto. He was going down the steps with Massey when they were hailed.

The voice came from a tall, florid, overweight youth with a black moustache and slightly prominent teeth, who sat behind the wheel of an open Bentley, its British racing green paint bright in the morning sun, its radiator and huge headlamps glittering. "Want a lift?"

Nobody wanted a lift from Flying Officer Blakeney-Smith, the egregious Simon, with all his money and conceit, his Turkish cigarettes and caddish civilian friends.

But he already had a passenger, whom it seemed churlish to leave alone with him. "Froggy" Dunal, the squadron's solitary Frenchman, who was too fastidious to welcome Blakeney-Smith's company, but too courteous to refuse the loutish young Englishman's invitation, gave the other two an appealing look. They climbed into the back of the 4½ litre passion wagon, Moonshine grumbling in disappointment, and let the lumpkin Simon drive them the half-mile or so around the perimeter track to the bays where the Hurricanes were sheltered.

Most of the aircraft stood outside their bays, facing the airfield and ready for take-off. There were no concrete or tarmac runways at East Malford, so once an aeroplane turned into wind it had virtually the whole width of the airfield open to it as long as there was a long enough run ahead.

At one end of each squadron's dispersal lines stood two or three huts, corrugated iron Nissens or standard Air Ministry wooden shacks. From one, which housed 172 pilots' crew room, a gramophone blared "I Don't Want To Set The World On Fire", while from another, where the workshop and ground crews' rest room were, a wireless set turned to full volume broadcast Vera Lynn belting out "We'll Meet Again". Like most of the Hurricanes on the dispersal line, both gramophone and radio were war-scarred.

Fitters, riggers and armourers added their voices to one or the other, creating the habitual cheerful din of British troops at work.

It was the usual start to any day on an operational fighter station.

SOME EIGHTY MILES TO THE SOUTH-EAST OF EAST Malford, Leutnant Erich Hafner was emerging from sleep at about the same time as Peter Knight, his enemy. But the hand on his shoulder was more delicate than Tuttle's and the voice in his ear more intimate.

Gentle fingers on his bare skin. "Time to wake, *mon trésor.*" The brush of soft lips on his cheek.

In an instant he passed from sleep to full wakefulness and opened his eyes wide. The girl lay with her naked breasts against his chest, her blonde hair falling about her pretty face. He put his arms around her and pulled her hard against him, so that she squealed and protested "Not now, *mon chou...* tonight... now you must be a good boy and get up." She wriggled free of his clasp and out of bed, giggling as she evaded his reaching hand. He lay admiring her while she put on her underclothes and slid her bare feet into shoes: silk stockings were too precious to risk laddering just to go home in the early morning; she put hers away in her handbag.

There was a knock on the door of the farmhouse bedroom and Hafner called "Come". Greiner, his servant, a serious looking man of thirty-five with flat feet, astigmatism and boundless sincerity, sidled in holding a tray bearing a large kettle of boiling water and two small cups of coffee.

The girl was washing at the enamel basin on a table in a corner of the room, regardless of the batman who was pottering about tidying. Hafner sipped his coffee, watched her with proprietary self-congratulation, then got out of bed, said "See you tonight," and went down to have his shower.

When II JG 97, No. 2 Gruppe of the 97th Jagd, or Fighter, Geschwader had come to this corner of northern France they had requisitioned farm buildings, village dwellings and large country houses: the officers and men in each of the three Staffelen in the Gruppe were billeted together; Oberleutnant Werner Richter's Staff el, in which Hafner flew, had taken over a big farm and its labourers' cottages. The bathing facilities were not up to the standard demanded by a German officer, so the parent Geschwader's engineers had rigged up showers under canvas shelters. There, on this fine July morning, young Erich Hafner met all his brother officers of the Staffel.

By the time he returned to his room, Greiner was standing to attention holding his shaving brush and soap. Whenever a girl stayed the night with his officer, Greiner made sure that she left enough water for him to shave comfortably after his shower. He believed that the commissioned ranks of the German armed forces were an élite even more exalted than the old nobility and that it was a privilege to serve them. He had an idealistic notion that the wild young lecher to whom he was orderly was a heroic demi-god, a winged Siegfried who rode the sky in defence of the Fatherland with gallant disregard for danger, trailing glory wherever he went. It did not disgust Greiner to launder Leutnant Hafner's soiled garments or mop up his vomit.

JG 97 had fought in Poland; but that campaign was over almost as soon as it started: and there had been little for the fighters to do, for it was a dive-bombers' war. Hafner had seen action but scored no victories in Poland.

But when the Geschwader began operating over France he made his first kill: a Potez, slow and helpless under the guns of his Me. 109. In the fighting that drove the British Expeditionary

Force to Dunkirk there were more worthy targets and in greater numbers. In those few weeks he shot down a Blenheim, a Fairey Battle, and, sharing this victory with two of his comrades, at last he brought down a Hurricane. A shared kill was not as satisfactory as one made in single combat, but at least he could now claim a British fighter among his few victims.

Since then he had flown more sorties than he could count without reference to his logbook; added two Moranes (targets as easy as the old Potez), two more Fairey Battles, another Blenheim and a Spitfire to his tally of kills; and damaged another Spitfire and a couple of Hurricanes. His own Me. 109 had been shot full of holes more than once. He had crash landed on a French beach. He had baled out when a Hurricane pilot set his Messerschmitt on fire, its engine stopped, with two well aimed bursts. He knew what it was to feel so frightened that he could not control his bladder or his bowels; what it was to see his comrades killed, wounded, blinded, maimed, drowned and burned beyond recognition.

He had come to this war with fewer illusions about the British than his friends had. Four years earlier, when he was eighteen, his swimming club's junior team had toured England, Scotland and Wales for three weeks, competing against schoolboys. There was always the same contrast in physique. He himself was a hulking, broad shouldered 160 lbs., as were most of his companions. The English, Welsh and Scots (decadent British youth!) were puny by comparison and twenty-five pounds lighter on average. But the Germans lost all but three of their twelve matches: at swimming and diving they were inferior to the scrawny British boys whose pale bodies contrasted so miserably with their own bronzed Aryan hides. Only at water polo, where beef does count, did they win half their games; but even so there was always some wily or invincibly determined young Briton to surprise them with long, devastating shots at goal from fantastic angles, or dogged and impenetrable defence against the most ferocious attacks.

Early in life Erich Hafner had learned that there is a hidden quality about the British which blunts the rapier thrusts and fends off the sledgehammer blows of the most formidable opponents. He thought it was mere stubbornness and cunning; if he lived to see the end of the war he might become wise enough to recognise it for what it really was: an undefeasible national spirit.

Respectfully Greiner asked: "Do you think the Tommies will give you a real fight today, Herr Leutnant?"

"Their orders are to leave us fighters alone and go for our bombers." Hafner explained this to his batman almost daily, but the reiteration did not bore him. It made him feel responsible, officer-like, quite paternal. "So we shall have to go after them, as usual."

"It will be a fine birthday present if the Führer awards you your Iron Cross in good time. That would please your parents and make them very proud."

True, it would make his father proud when he won his first decoration. He knew that his father wished he had been born to look like the pure young Aryan he was, inheriting his own fair Saxon colouring instead of taking after his dark Bavarian mother. With deep brown eyes and hair that was almost black, Hafner could, with his perenially sunbronzed face, have passed for an Italian; the ultimate insult. But it must give some comfort to that stolid Düsseldorf banker, with his own Iron Cross from the Kaiser's war on display in his library, that his eldest son was an officer in the glorious Luftwaffe which had blasted the Blitzkrieg triumphantly across Poland, the Low Countries and France at breathtaking speed.

"Yes, it would please my parents, old Greiner. But it would please me even more." He grinned, dabbing the last few flecks of soap from his face with a fresh towel.

"It will happen before the end of the month, Herr Leutnant." It was a confident prediction.

Suddenly the pilot scowled. He found himself trembling. His airman's superstition responded instantly to such statements. "Damn you, don't you know better than to tempt providence like that? Are you trying to bring me bad luck, you damned idiot?"

"F-f-forgive me Herr Leutnant. I d-d-didn't think…"

"Then *do* think in future. Think carefully before you utter idiocies about things of which you know nothing." Hafner held out his hand. "Where is it?"

"In your pocket sir, as always."

"Shew it to me. You are careless enough to forget to put it where it belongs." An unjust accusation.

The batman was fumbling with a button. "Here… here it is, s-sir."

Hafner snatched the medallion which lay on the palm of Greiner's shaking hand and fingered it for a moment with his eyes shut. He thrust the tawdry souvenir of a childhood visit to the Vatican back into the pocket of his tunic which Greiner held out to him. It was his talisman, his lucky piece, without which he would never fly. His mother had made him promise always to carry it. It was better, he told himself, to be superstitious about a holy medal than about the pagan symbols on which most of his friends relied: silk stockings peeled from the legs of chorus girls, "lucky" cigarette lighters, scarves, charm bracelets, girls' photographs, seashells or rabbits' feet. Most airmen put their trust in some token or totem or piece of mumbo-jumbo to keep them unscathed.

He felt sourly upset by Greiner's tactlessness and his own outburst of panicky bad temper. To cover his superstitious fear and his shame of it he asked frozenly "Where's Wolf?"

"Outside, Herr Leutnant, enjoying the sun." Greiner smiled tentatively.

Hafner went to the window and looked down into the farmyard. His Alsatian dog sprawled in a sheltered comer, basking in the already warm sunlight When he spent the night with a girl he made the dog sleep downstairs. Now he leaned out and called and instantly the great black and tawny animal bounded up, its ears pricked, and raced for the door. He waited with an expectant smile and braced himself to meet the staggering force of that powerful body as Wolf leaped up to place forepaws on his shoulders and nuzzle him wetly.

Good humour restored, Hafner swaggered down to breakfast in the villa two hundred meters away which the Staff el Commander, Oberleutnant Werner Richter, had taken for himself, his adjutant and his two most senior officers, one a pilot and the other an engineer.

It was in this house that all the officers of the Staffel assembled for meals and recreation. They always referred to it as the mess, never the C.O's quarters. Richter liked it that way: it implied a comradeship which did not set him apart from the officers he commanded.

Hafner knocked on doors as he passed them on his way out of the farmhouse and three other young pilots joined him; a couple more had already left.

They paused on the steps of the mess and surveyed the sky. At an immense altitude overhead, so high and so small that even they, with their airmen's eyes, could barely make out the glint of reflected light that betrayed it, flew an unidentifiable aircraft.

"Tommy taking photographs," someone commented.

"With luck, they'll come and bomb the airfield," remarked Hafner. "That's the only way we'll ever get it levelled out."

The others laughed at the witty chap. They all disliked the undulating meadowland which was not a proper aerodrome at all. They were used to good concrete runways in the Fatherland.

They felt no ill-will towards the Englishman up there in his high flying photographic reconnaissance Spitfire. Sooner or later someone would shoot him down. In the meantime he was doing his job and not harming them directly. War was ruthless but one could be fair, after all. And everything was on their side: they had more aircraft and more pilots than the R.A.F. They had confidence, with victory in continental Europe already theirs. The initiative lay in their hands: they were attacking and forcing Britain to defend herself. To attack meant to be strong. Defence was a position of weakness.

The only real anxiety of Leutnant Erich Hafner and his comrades was that the British would probably be conquered so swiftly that they would be denied the high score of victories they all craved.

.

WHEN 172 SQUADRON CAME ON DUTY, NO. 82, WHO had been on readiness since dawn, went back to their messes for breakfast. An hour later they would return to readiness. On the far side of the airfield No. 699, an Auxiliary Air Force squadron, could he heard warming up their Hurricanes preparatory to going up on sector reconnaissance: the usual routine for newly arrived pilots, to familiarise themselves with landmarks which would help them to find their way back to base in bad weather or when their compasses or radios were shot away. They had flown in the day before from a quiet airfield in the north and had never yet been in action.

The pilots of 172 Squadron settled down, with their "Mae West" life vests on, to sleep, read or merely sit and think; or perhaps try not to. Some found chairs, others stretched out on the grass.

At any moment, they knew, would come a ring on the telephone which would send them running to their cockpits. Two minutes later they would be on their way to meet the enemy. Within an hour after that they would be back; some of them. Of those who did not return, a few would arrive eventually after being picked up in the Channel or escaping from their wrecked aircraft in a field or on a beach. But many of them would never be seen again on the squadron; if they were not killed, they would be badly injured. It would be like that all day: three… four… even six scrambles; and of the pilots who waited at readiness, not all would surely be there at stand-down.

They tried to relax while remaining alert enough to leap to their feet and break into a run immediately the telephone orderly or whoever happened to be nearest to the telephone shouted "Scramble!"

Squadron Leader Maxwell, their C.O., who had gone straight to the squadron hangar when he arrived on camp from his rented house nearby, arrived on the heels of his squadron in his elderly Morris Oxford.

"A" Flight commander, Flight Lieutenant "Jumper" Lee, was with him. The R.A.F. likes to bestow nicknames. F. Lee made flea, and fleas jump; hence "Jumper".

Those pilots who had their eyes open said "Good morning, sir," to Maxwell. The rest, even if they heard the C.O. arrive, did not show any signs of life. Nobody even pretended to rise: the C.O. had told them that they were not to waste their energy in paying him courtesies which were all very well in normal times but a fatuous charade these days.

Maxwell was dapper, leisurely and thirty-one. His flight commanders were seven or eight years younger and the rest of the squadron averaged twenty-one. His greatest worry was that if the Germans bombed the aerodrome, his wife and small son would be endangered: their present home was only two miles away. He sometimes became anxious about promotion; he did not want it. Commanding a squadron was the best job in the Air Force. Higher rank took one away from the rare and intensely individual comradeship of the smallest fighting unit and further from the most intimate involvement in battle. Worse than promotion would be a posting to instruct at a flying school or on an operational training unit. He dismissed this with one of his wry jokes: teaching new pilots was likely to be more dangerous than fighting the Germans.

He went into his office at one end of the wooden hut which housed the crew room: on the faded grey-blue door "C.O." was painted in black. These days one economised in everything, he reflected, even paint. Lee followed him in.

Tossing his cap on to the table, Maxwell asked "Where's Spike?"

Lee paused in the doorway, looked towards the somnolent or preoccupied figures outside and shouted "Spike! Anyone seen…?"

Somebody called "He's over by his aircraft, binding his fitter."

Two or three of the pilots and several of the ground crew within hearing laughed. Flight Lieutenant "Spike" Poynter, commanding "B" Flight, was notorious for his fervid interest in internal combustion engines and the cars and aircraft they propelled. A keen rally driver in peacetime, he spent much time in discussion with his fitter, rigger and flight mechanic. He was somewhere down the dispersal line now, talking about some fancied drop in oil pressure or imagined defect in the magneto of his perfectly sound Hurricane.

Lee told a nearby aircrafthand to fetch Flight Lieutenant Poynter and the airman doubled off. All the troops doubled when Jumper gave an order; not because he was a martinet, but because he was popular. He had won a D.F.C. over France, shot down nine enemy aircraft, with three probables, could drink eight pints of beer between stand-down and bed-time without turning a hair, and took a different girl to bed every week; so the erks liked, envied and admired him. He was not badly thought of by the other pilots, either.

Squadron Leader Maxwell's first and last duties of the day were his visits to the squadron hangar. Here, technical tradesmen who were seldom seen out at the dispersal area, yet were an essential part of the squadron, toiled long hours and achieved miracles.

He went to see them and their work as much to give praise and encouragement, and the reassurance that they belonged to a fighting unit which valued their skills highly, as to take an account of how many aircraft he would have for that day or the next.

The battle had become a matter not only of making the best use of the comparatively few experienced pilots, training the novices, and putting them all into the air so as to be in the right place at the right time, but of finding enough aeroplanes for them to fly and shoot from. He marvelled every day at the transformations he saw: badly mauled Hurricanes, holed, dented, twisted and scorched, restored overnight to flying condition by weary, red-eyed, oil-blackened and cheerfully grousing technicians who often worked twenty-four hours without sleep. He was always astonished that the harder they worked the better humoured they seemed to be.

He picked up some papers from his desk and read them impatiently, while Lee, with his rolling gait, waist and chest proportioned like a beer barrel, carrying himself always very erect to make the most of his five-feet-eight, padded back and forth between the windows which looked on to different parts of the aerodrome, scanning sky and field critically as the newly arrived 699 Squadron went about their lawful occasions. Now and again he exclaimed "Kee-rist!" or "Stap me!" at a bouncy landing or a delayed raising of wheels.

There was a knock on the door and Spike Poynter came briskly in, his sharp, pink face alert and head thrust forward like an eager sparrow's. " 'Morning, sir. Flap on?"

Maxwell put down the letters and notices in his hand with relief. "Only normal flap, Spike. Jumper and I've just been to the hangar. We should have two more serviceable by lunch time. Tell your boys to keep their fingers out: there are supposed to be replacements coming in any day, but at this rate we won't be able to keep on putting up twelve serviceable aircraft."

"Aircraft state" was the daily bugbear of all commanders. The group captain commanding the station worried about it above all else, for without enough aircraft to fight with, East Malford would be impotent. The squadron commanders, harassed by casualties among their pilots, every one of which struck home to even the least emotional or sentimental of them as though he had lost a brother, were obsessed with the paramount need to patch up and make do, to keep Hurricanes which were veterans of too many battles still in a state to fly. They rode their Squadron Engineer Officers hard and knew that they would pass this necessary persecution down to their flight sergeants.

Maxwell and his flight commanders discussed the squadron's aircraft state, the pilot strength, the battle training they must give the newly joined pilots; which meant risking the loss of, or damage to, badly needed aircraft as well as human casualties. They talked about the need to provide more rest for the maintenance crews and ways and means of squeezing in a day or two of leave for as many of them as could be filched from the hangar or the dispersal bays, a few at a time, without giving the "plumber" (the engineer officer) apoplexy.

They talked about tactics and the weather and the imminence of a German invasion; they telephoned the Operations Room to ask if any enemy raids were plotted; they cursed the momentary inactivity, while counting it a boon that gave them more time to bring their aircraft up to greater strength. Then the Squadron Adjutant arrived on his bicycle from the squadron office in the hangar, with files for the C.O., and Lee and Poynter picked up their caps and went outside to flop out on the grass with the rest.

They listened to Flight Sergeant Viccar, known naturally as "The Bishop" or "Bish", telling indignantly about the cold reception given to N.C.O. pilots who were posted to Auxiliary Air Force squadrons. His wavy, oiled black hair and spiky moustache gave him a piratical, rather than an ecclesiastical, air.

"This V.R. sergeant on 699 was telling me in the mess last night, they only have commissioned pilots in the Auxiliaries..."

"So why would Volunteer Reserve sergeant pilots be posted to an auxiliary squadron?" asked Massey.

Viccar, the most immaculate dresser on 172, adjusted his trouser creases and the fold of his carefully ironed, brightly coloured, silk square. "Because there aren't any V.R. squadrons. V.R. pilots are in a kind of pool. They're week-end pilots, like the auxiliaries, but they're not organised the same. When the war started, they had to be posted to squadrons: the lucky ones came to regular squadrons, but the other poor blighters went to auxiliary squadrons. This type was telling me the more flying hours the V.R.s have the more the auxiliaries hate them, like. He says he'd rather shoot some of *them* down than a Jerry, any day."

"And that's been done before now," observed Knight; not without relish; and a thoughtful glance at Blakeney-Smith.

He had been dozing comfortably for the past half-hour and now that Flight Sergeant Viccar's critical voice had roused him he opened his eyes and looked round for his dog. Moonshine lay at his feet, ears pricked and watching his face for signs of waking. As soon as his master stirred, Moonshine took a flying leap on to his chest and enthusiastically thrust his wet muzzle into Knight's chin. He was allowed to stay there.

Knight and Massey played a private game, much enjoyed by the spectators but never intruded in. It was Six-gun's invention, with the alleged purpose of keeping his friend's and his own reactions sharp. Awake now, Knight at once cocked a wary eye for signs of sudden movement from Six-gun. The rules of the game were simple enough; banal, Blakeney-Smith said. Without warning, one of them would throw something at the other, with a shout of "Catch!" Whoever was the receiver had to look sharp or some solid object was likely to strike him in a tender spot; enamel mugs, cricket balls, books, empty bottles or even an apple or orange were all capable of leaving their mark; and frequently did.

Stealthily, while apparently absorbed in The Bishop's diatribe, which was (as usual with the rumours and accusations circulated by Other Ranks, compounded of a nucleus of fact smothered by a vast amount of embroidery), Massey had taken from his pocket a large bone he had bribed Tuttle to obtain from the mess kitchen the night before.

With a yell of "Catch!" he launched it in Knight's direction. Caught off guard, the latter twisted under Moonshine's weight and flung out both arms in an attempt to catch the missile. The dog, with a yelp of excitement, dug his hind feet into Knight's chest and took off in a flying leap to try to intercept the bone. The powerful thrust upset the balance of Knight, who had already partly risen. For a moment there was a confusion of arms, legs, barking, a bounding dog and an officer tipped out of his deck chair. The chair collapsed on top of Knight; and Moonshine, now yapping hysterically with joy, managed to get himself trapped between his master's chest and the grass as he scrabbled excitedly to cover the last few inches which separated him from the prize.

The noise and confusion woke all those who were still sleeping and brought officers and men tumbling out of rest huts and workshops.

The C.O. took three strides to his door, flung it open and stood transfixed, as bug-eyed as though the Germans had dropped a battalion of parachutists on East Malford. When he saw Knight on the ground, apparently engaged in a wrestling bout with his dog, and Six-gun doing a war dance around them and the flattened deck chair, while making derisive and victorious noises, Squadron Leader Maxwell joined in the general laughter.

He was grateful for Massey's clowning and endless high spirits: they took the tenseness out of his pilots' faces and, for a moment, they had forgotten everything in the relief of hearty amusement. It was the basic humorous situation that never failed; the slip on the banana skin, the prat-fall.

Knight picked himself up and, poker-faced, allowing his friend no satisfaction, began brushing grass from his clothes. With feigned disgust, he said "That wasn't cricket. Setting a man's own dog on him is against the rules…"

Massey jeered. "You wanna pull your finger out…"

The noise of the telephone ringing in the crew room rose above the voices and the laughing. Seconds later the orderly yelled, from the door, " "A" Flight scramble!"

A/C1 Tuttle, N. was, for the moment, happy in his work. He walked along the road from the Officers' Mess to his billet, whistling.

He passed the officers' tennis court and approached the first of the Officers' Married Quarters. This house, bigger than the others, was occupied in peacetime by the Station Commander. There was a double row of other large, red brick houses, each standing in about a sixth of an acre of garden. A hundred yards beyond the last of these the road turned at a right angle and the Airmen's Married Quarters began: small, terraced dwellings in blocks of four. No families, officers' or other ranks', occupied married quarters now: all had been evacuated when war was declared, to make room for the many more men and women who would be posted in to bring the station up to wartime strength. Normally there were only two squadrons at East Malford, whereas there were now three. The barrack blocks on the main camp could not accommodate the extra numbers, so families had to leave.

The W.A.A.F officers lived in the former Station Commander's house, and it was there that Tuttle was bound.

Over his arm he carried an officer pilot's tunic; Flying Officer Knight's. If anyone in authority had asked him where he was going, he would have lied that he was taking it to the camp tailor for repair.

A pilot's uniform was essential to his scheme for ensuring himself an admiring welcome from the factory and shop girls of his native city on his next leave.

One of the other batmen, who shared his room in Airmen's M.Q., owned a camera; and also suffered from a sense of inferiority when competing for civilian feminine favours. Tuttle, slipping half a pound of stolen Officers' Mess butter across the counter with his money, had been able to buy one of the few rolls of film that the village chemist had in stock.

This morning each was to take photographs of the other wearing Knight's best blue tunic. When they next went on leave they intended to wear civilian clothes (Tuttle was a notably sharp dresser), explain modestly that they liked to get out of uniform for a complete break from the horrors of war, and show photographs of themselves disguised as officer pilots to confirm their claims to death-defying valour in the cockpit of a fighter.

Tuttle was a hefty middleweight with a brawny physique built by weightlifting. He was a moderately successful amateur boxer and not above taking a clandestine fiver to box professionally when he had the chance. Being of the same build as Knight, the latter's tunic fitted him well. His friend, who worked for some administrative officers living in married quarters, had no opportunity to borrow a pilot's uniform and would have to put up with whatever Tuttle could procure; which was unfortunate, because he was thin and stunted. Tuttle, however, had assured him that Knight's tunic would fit him a treat.

The photographic deception was not the only reason for Tuttle to be whistling as he sauntered most unmilitarily along. He was a good-looking youth, in a red-faced and greasy-haired fashion, with a knowing city way about him which appealed to the younger and more impressionable airwomen. The W.A.A.F. officers who lived in No. 1 O.M.Q. were served by two batwomen. The elder of these was already being provided with an active sex life by one of the ground officers billeted further down the road. The other, a farm girl of more humble aspirations, was a new arrival and only eighteen years old. Tuttle was after her rustic virginity; and confident of success between now and next pay day, which was a fortnightly event.

He still had fourteen shillings left from his last pay day, six days ago, and there were weekly tips from his officers: so it was not as though he had nothing to offer but his charm. He was a suitor of comparative substance, although batmen were lowly-paid and handicapped when rivalling technical tradesmen for female attention.

With the tunic which was to be his magic cloak tucked under his arm, his forage cap tilted so far to the right that only his cauliflower ear prevented it falling off, one hand in his pocket and the other holding one of the Turkish cigarettes he stole every day from Simon Blakeney-Smith's room, he turned down the path to the back door of O.M.Q.1, anticipating a prettily blushing welcome, a cosy cup of tea with a slice of buttered toast and jam, and a few minutes' amorous mauling.

He was half-way down the path to the back door when six Hurricanes roared overhead with a noise like a hundred double-decker buses (Tuttle was a bus conductor in civilian life). He stood and craned his head back to watch them. He recognised the letters of 172 Squadron on one side of the fuselage roundels. On the other side of its roundel the leading aircraft in the second section bore the letter "E": that was Knight's kite, he told himself. So "A" Flight had been scrambled, had they? No hurry with the tunic, then.

Them pilots was a lot of mugs, he thought with satisfaction. They spent all day out at dispersals, waiting with their nerves jangling for the scramble order to come. They flew and flew again, until they were so bleedin' weary they could hardly stay awake. They got shot at, wounded, burned, killed. And all for what? With the same objective at the end of the day as he had after spending it in safety and comfort between the mess, his billet and the W.A.A.F. Officers' quarters. While Knight and the rest of them flew their arses off (and got them shot off, too), he had a nice kip on his bed every afternoon; and often shared it with one of the off-duty W.A.A.F. But in the evening, when they were finished with work, they were all after the same thing: taking a tart down the boozer for a pint and a song around the piano, then "avin" it off in an air raid shelter or a haystack on the way back to camp.

Tuttle knew who the mugs were in this war.

BREAKFAST FOR THE OFFICERS OF NO. 1 STAFFEL, II JG 97, was rich with the spoils of conquest. In the Fatherland they were used to poor bread, no butter, dubious sausage and imitation coffee. Here in France they sat down to huge, swollen omelettes, good dairy butter, warm loaves and delicious coffee.

It was a noisy meal, accompanied by much arrogant talk full of bravado. Everyone said how he hoped the R.A.F. fighters would give battle that day instead of ignoring the Messerschmitt escort and attacking the bombers. The top cover German fighters were under orders to stay in position. Only those who gave close escort to the bombers had a chance of mixing it with the Hurricanes and Spitfires. The daily breakfast time topic was how the Luftwaffe would clear the skies within the next few days so that the Wehrmacht could invade England.

As each officer entered the dining room he clicked his heels and bowed to Oberleutnant Richter at the head of the table. Leutnant Erich Hafner, like his crony Otto Ihlefeld, always ate well when he had been with a woman. They had been together at training school and each now led a Schwarm of four aircraft. There were three Schwärme in a Staffel.

The Gruppe to which they belonged was commanded by a major and comprised three Staffelen. No. 1 Staffel's Commanding Officer had fought for the Fascists in Spain and taken part in the rape of Poland and the Blitzkrieg on Holland, Belgium and France. To his pilots he was a kind of deity. To himself he was a worried family man with a fatherlike responsibility for sixteen young fliers. The Gruppe Commander, who not only had three Staffelen but some fifty pilots to cause him ulcers and sleepless nights, understood the problems of his Staffel commanders and often invited them to his chateau to get drunk and go to bed with French whores fetched from Paris, discreetly out of sight of their juniors. As Richter was not over-fond of women, he appreciated the thought rather more than the deed. If the Gruppe Commander would invite him to bring apple-cheeked young Leutnant Hans Baumbach along for the night, now, that would be another matter. A willowy ex-ballet dancer, Oberfeldwebel Franz Helbig, appealed to him most strongly; but these affairs were always difficult to arrange between an officer and an N.C.O. And if one did succeed, the boys were apt to be presumptuous, ultimately, with their smirking requests for leave and other favours.

Richter greeted each of his officers with a cold nod and a curt word of response. One or two of the more ardent Hitler-worshippers among them used to have the habit of slamming their boots together in the doorway and shooting their arms out in a Nazi salute with a cry of "Heil Hitler!" But he had soon put a stop to that: it was more than could be expected of a man, to keep interrupting his morning victuals by flinging his arm out galvanically and mumbling "Heil Hitler" through a mouthful of omelette and croissant. Besides, all that stamping and boot-bashing sent a bolt of pain through his head after a night at the chateau.

Oberleutnant Richter was a tall, heavily built, blond man of twenty-eight; a ski-ing champion, a noted yachtsman (he enjoyed the intimacy of small cabins) and a keen wrestler. Women fell in love with him on sight and embarrassed him with their attentions. In an attempt to conceal his tastes from his comrades he accepted female adulation, while admitting frankly that he was not a tit-man or a leg-man but an admirer of a tight little butt. His pilots accepted this mild aberration as a normal stag eccentricity and any girl with a trim pair of buttocks was regarded as "the C.O.'s meat" and duly presented to him.

There was talk up and down the table of the day's prospects. The Staffel was proud of its Me. 109s but jealous of the Spitfires. Hurricanes were another matter: slower than the Messerschmitts, they were believed to be comparatively easy victims; and would have been a lot easier if they were not so bravely and brilliantly flown and strongly built. Two-thirds of Fighter Command's squadrons were, the German pilots knew, equipped with Hurricanes and only one-third with Spitfires. Each of them secretly wondered what the Luftwaffe's chances of success would be if the proportions were reversed.

Meanwhile the invasion barges had been assembled along the coast of the Pas de Calais and the area was swarming with infantry, ready to go aboard in their life jackets and leap ashore on the beaches of southern England. Once there, they would soon be marching up Whitehall while the Luftwaffe celebrated with drinks in the R.A.F. Club in Piccadilly.

To make it all possible the German fighters first had to sweep the Spitfires and Hurricanes out of the sky and the German bombers to put the R.A.F. fighter airfields and coastal radar stations out of action. They had to destroy every British fighter within range which was left on the ground. Only then could the barges laden with assault troops set out.

The pilots of Richter's Staffel talked hopefully about how the R.A.F. would have to come up and fight when the bomber formations crossed the English coast; and then the escorting Me. 109s would tear them to pieces. Only let them come up and meet us! they prayed. And they meant it.

Sometimes Hafner remembered his three weeks in Britain as an eighteen-year-old swimmer. He recalled how he and his team mates had laughed when they first saw their British adversaries strip; and how their pride in their physical superiority had been humbled when they lost one contest after another. The modesty of those British youngsters often came to his mind and sounded a warning: some of them must be flying the Spitfires and Hurricanes that met him and his comrades every day over the Channel, the Sussex Downs and the hop-fields of Kent; the fighters which had brought death and disfigurement to so many of the Gruppe already.

He wondered about the high-spirited boy with whom he had made friends, exchanged visits and, for a couple of years, maintained a correspondence. He could remember him clearly, even after the lapse of four years: his physique was better than average and he had the fair hair and blue eyes which Hafner's own father would have wished for his son. They had met when the German team competed against one of the famous English public schools: a place Hafner recalled as a rambling, ivy-covered group of ancient buildings set in beautiful countryside, where the boys were cut off for eight months of the year from any contact with the opposite sex. Very different from the Third Reich, where Hitler's boys and girls were encouraged to go camping and nude sun-bathing and swimming together and let nature take its delightful course.

The strong, fair-haired boy was swimming captain of his school, and because Hafner was captain of the German team he was invited to tea in the English boy's study; they had liked each other and exchanged addresses. Letters followed, and then an invitation to Hafner to spend a fortnight in the English boy's home: the father was a doctor in a pleasant Berkshire town, and there were two younger brothers and a younger sister. It was a happy, hospitable family and Erich Hafner had enjoyed himself. Then, in the winter, he invited his English friend to come ski-ing with his own family for two weeks in the Bavarian mountains.

Soon after that they both became air force pilots. But instead of creating a further bond it had separated them; German politics were not popular in Britain and regular officers looked askance at the rapidly growing forces of the Third Reich.

Gazing across the narrow Straits of Dover, Leutnant Hafner often wondered whether Peter Knight were among those waiting on the other side to kill him.

"A" Flight of 172 Squadron returned singly within an hour of taking off.

Maxwell and the rest of the squadron who were at dispersals, ground crews as well as pilots and the Squadron Intelligence Officer, counted them in.

Since they had heard Lee call "Tallyho! Individual attacks… Go!" on the R/T set in the crew room, there had been no message from Knight's No. 2 man, Pierre Dunal.

There was silence while all eyes searched the sky. Dunal was not the only pilot who had not yet returned. Then came the rumble of a Merlin engine in the distance and a few seconds later "E", with four black, white-outlined German crosses painted on its nose, with a small white dog chewing a swastika-shaped bone alongside them, zoomed low over the boundary hedge.

The Hurricane came bumping and swaying over the grass, Knight cut the engine, clambered down from the cockpit and forestalled the obvious question by calling out "Froggy's O.K. I saw him bale out near Folkestone. Landed on the beach. Some brown jobs were waiting for him. He'll be back any minute."

Lee said grimly "He needn't hurry: he hasn't got an aircraft."

One of the squadron's two Polish pilots, "Lottie" Lotnikski, said something to his compatriot which no one understood but the purport of which was quite clear.

Knight turned on him. "It's all very well for you to bind about his losing an aircraft, Lottie, but you weren't there. We ran into twenty-four of the sods, escorting sixteen Heinkels. What the hell were we supposed to do? We tried to go for the bombers, but the 109s kept boring in. I saw Pierre get a Heinkel before three of them bounced him."

The Pole made no reply. He and his countryman exchanged glances and shrugged. Nobody was going to change their view of the French Armée de l'Air. They and the rest of the surviving pilots in their squadron of the Polish Air Force had trekked across Hungary, Roumania, Bulgaria and Greece, subject to every kind of hardship and humiliation, and made their way to France to continue the fight. They had found a cynical, disillusioned French Air Force, reconciled to the inevitability of defeat and reluctant to fly. They had kicked their heels on French Military airfields, begging to be allowed to use the idle fighters which stood on the tarmac while most French pilots drank cognac all day and a few flew like haggard demons, trying to save their country's honour even though they had no hope of averting its fate.

The French had treated the Poles with suspicion at best, usually with contempt. Commandants and colonels had told them unpleasantly that they had already proved their worthlessness when the Luftwaffe crushed them in five weeks. What they did not take into account, and probably did not even know, was that the 200 out-dated fighters of the Polish Air Force had shot down 250 of the 2,000 German bombers and fighters which had swarmed over their country. Nor did the French admit that perhaps they themselves would have been battered to extinction already but for the presence of twenty-nine R.A.F. squadrons, eleven of them fighters, on French soil.

The Poles, burning with resentment, shame and anger, were spoiling for a fight. The French sneered that they had been shewn to be no good at fighting; and did not know how to fly French aircraft types anyway.

So eventually the Poles got to England and were welcomed in the R.A.F.; and allowed to fly the best fighters the British had.

Pilot Officer Lotnikski had not yet developed much *esprit de corps* towards his squadron comrade Lieutenant Dunal. Perhaps understandably. Dunal avoided speaking to him or the other Polish pilot. And perhaps that was understandable too.

Pilot Officer "Spy Herrick, the Intelligence Officer, looked up from the form on which he was writing. "Any joy, Peter?"

Knight's rigger brought him a mug of tea, and between gulps he said "When we broke I dived on a Heinkel in the centre of the second vie and gave him a four-second burst from the port quarter. His port engine started to smoke…" And so it went on, each pilot's story the same: attacks on bombers which had to be broken off to deal with the fighter escort before the Heinkels could be destroyed. Their orders were to attack the bombers and leave the German fighters alone, but the Me. 109s wouldn't leave them alone and too many bombers were still getting through.

At the end of it the I.O. reckoned up two Heinkel Ills destroyed and three damaged, and one Messerschmitt shot down.

Two of the returned Hurricanes had bullet holes but were fit to fly again as soon as they had been refuelled and rearmed.

It was an encouraging start to the day's work. 172's "A" Flight pilots reclined in their chairs and went on talking among themselves about the first sortie, their hands moving to simulate aircraft attitudes, their voices rising as they talked each other down.

"B" Flight, whose turn it was to scramble next, unless the whole squadron were ordered up, were quiet and alert.

A slow, high-winged aircraft that looked like a dragon-fly flopped on to the airfield, taxied over to 172's dispersal and stopped. Pierre Dunal emerged from it He looked sheepish as he strolled over to the Intelligence Officer but tried to be nonchalant in the R.A.F. style.

He went straight to his flight commander. "I am sorry, Jumpair. I tried to shake them off, but there are three of them on my tail, and...." He shrugged expressively.

Lee replied quietly "All right, Pierre, I saw what happened. But don't make a habit of it: we haven't got the aircraft to spare."

Maxwell, from the door of his office, holding a file in his hand, waved his pipe to attract the Frenchman's attention. Dunal walked quickly over and stood at attention.

"I am sorry, Sair…"

"Glad to see you back, Pierre. Are you fit?"

"Yes, thank you, Sair. I am ready for the next scramble…"

Maxwell smiled. "You may be, but the aircraft state isn't. Take it easy for a couple of hours." He nodded amiably and withdrew indoors.

Herrick beckoned to Dunal and they walked away to find a quiet spot.

Knight had been interrupted three times in questioning Blakeney-Smith since they had landed. At that stage of the war, fighters flew in sections of three: Red and Yellow Sections making up "A" Flight, and Blue and Green, "B". The members of a section identified themselves, on the radio, by their section colour and a number. Thus, the leader of Yellow section was "Yellow 1"; his right and left wing men were, respectively, "Yellow 2" and "Yellow 3". The composition of sections was changed frequently; not only because casualties compelled this, but to train leaders.

On the last sortie, Knight was leading Yellow Section, with Dunal as Number Two. Blakeney-Smith, who was an experienced leader himself, was Number Three, charged with the duty of staying with Dunal if the latter became separated from the leader.

Now Knight was asking, for the third time, "What the hell happened to you, Simon? I told you to stick to Pierre like glue if he lost me. If you can't do better than that, with your experience as a section leader, you ought to go back to a training unit…"

"Don't be so damn pompous." Blakeney-Smith was lighting a cheroot and his voice was offensively muffled.

"If Froggy's ever going to lead a section, he needs confidence; and I don't think you helped."

"I can't wet nurse sprogs when I've got four 109s on my own tail, Peter."

"*I* didn't see them. And I didn't see you anywhere around when I tried to cover him myself."

"Don't tell *me* what you didn't see, chum. They were there. If you didn't see them, you need your eyes tested: so tell the doc, not me."

It was, as always, impossible to pin down the slippery Simon. You could hack away at him and he'd deflect the blows with his enormous shield of evasiveness.

Jumper Lee broke in. "Next sortie, Simon, you'll be Number Two to Pete: Six-gun'll fly Number Three; *you* learn to hang on to your leader."

Blakeney-Smith glared at his flight commander but said nothing. The implication of being kept under observation was best dismissed quickly.

Dunal came to sit next to Knight, who asked "Did you get a good look at the leader of those three 109s that jumped you?"

"Too good a look, *cher ami!*"

"He had a wolfs head painted on his kite."

"I was not looking for… for… *blasons*… badges, I assure you: I do not think I would have recognised my own mother in those moments, I was concentrating so much on… on other matters."

"I've seen that blighter before. He's got a black wolf's head on his cowling, with blood dripping from its jaws: very melodramatic and line-shooting. It's time someone put him out of business. I got a quick squirt at him, but then three more of them took a dirty dart at me and I thought it was time to give priority to a spot of self-preservation instead of gawping at Jerry art. That wolf thing annoys me like hell; it's such a line." In the pre-war peacetime air force, boasting, showing off, shooting a line, carried special penalties: such as de-bagging, being thrown into the river, finding one's room turned upside down. Knight had been conditioned to regard it as the most unofficer-like, and therefore ungentlemanly, of offences. He had a defiant emblem painted on his own aircraft, but it was humorous rather than vain-glorious.

He looked at Blakeney-Smith, who, with his tunic off, had his head tilted back to expose his face to the sun, cheroot between his teeth. "You'd better take care that Jerry wolf doesn't do a Little Red Riding Hood on *you*, Simon."

Then Peter Knight fell asleep in his chair.

IT WAS GOOD TO BE BACK ON THE GROUND AGAIN alive and unhurt That Hurricane which came so fast out of the sun had put a burst right through his cockpit: he could hear the wicked whine of the bullets now as they had sounded when they ripped through the metal and barely missed his suddenly cringing flesh. Erich Hafner wiped a handkerchief across his forehead as he stood with his comrades on the coarse meadow grass. Three of them had formed up over the Channel and landed together. They had seen the fourth member of the Schwarm go down in flames over England. Hafner said "By God! We hit the Tommies hard this time. Did anyone see Heinrich get out?"

The other two shook their heads.

They were standing by Hafner's aircraft. His mechanic was putting a finger into each of the bullet holes and exclaiming. Hafner watched for a moment, then said nonchalantly, "Unless it was sheer hick, that Tommy pilot wasn't bad." He held up his arm and shewed them where the cloth of his flying suit was torn. "At least one of his shots came fairly close."

Laughing, his friends linked arms with him and together the three of them strode towards the tents on the edge of the airfield.

Oberleutnant Richter, who had landed first, watched them approaching and his heart went out to them. He felt proud and possessive and privileged to lead them. He loved them all; and if it was with as much carnality as admiration and protectiveness, perhaps he was all the better commander for that. Most men would condemn his emotion as a weakness, but he was sure that it gave him a greater sensitivity to their feelings than other commanders could have. At the same time he knew that if his pilots ever suspected his true nature they would turn from him in disgust. If the Oberstleutnant (lieutenant-colonel) commanding the Geschwader were to recognise it he would lose his command of the Staffel at once and for ever. The strain of concealment was almost as great as the tension of battle and caring about his young men.

Grouped around him, the rest of the Staffel talked excitedly and gesticulated, shewing how they had attacked, been attacked, taken evasive action. In the midst of it all their Intelligence Officer, a harassed-looking ex-schoolmaster, sought myopically to make notes and extract coherent stories from them. He and Herrick would have sympathised with each other instinctively: they had the same problems; condensing and clarifying the recollections of exuberant youths into the dry formulae of intelligence reports was never easy, and often irritating; but, unlike the pilots, they were not allowed to display their temperament.

With sympathy, Richter caught his eye and smiled. Then spoke to the three last to land: "What happened to Heinrich, boys? Did you see him go down, Erich? Did he get out?"

Hafner made a gesture of disgust. "It was a Hurricane with a mongrel painted on it, chewing a bone… a swastika-shaped bone, the blasphemous swine. It got on his tail and put two long bursts into his engine before we could get there. I've seen that bastard before. He had four victories painted on his aeroplane already. Five is too many. I know his markings too: YZ-E. I'm going to keep a special watch for him." He paused, "Where's Horst?"

"Missing," replied Richter shortly and walked away.

Hafner looked up at the sky. "No sign of a break in the weather. Let's get at the *Scheissenkärle* again. What are our bomber boys waiting for? We can give them all the protection they need. Or do they want better odds than five to one?"

Otto Ihlefeld suggested "Perhaps they're afraid of the British *flak*."

That made everyone laugh. They had all seen Hurricanes and Spitfires caught in British anti-aircraft fire over England and by the guns of British naval vessels escorting Channel convoys. It was a standing joke that the German bombers had less to fear from the British Army and naval anti-aircraft gunners than the British fighters had.

Corporal Connie Gates was a batwoman/waitress of rare beauty. In any situation her face and figure would have turned men's heads and aroused the envy of other women. She had won beauty contests and been carnival queen of the Devon seaside town where she was born and raised. After a monotonous life of work in hotel dining rooms she had married a junior merchant marine officer. Five years later, as soon as she had sped him on his way in the first convoy for the Far East, she had joined the W.A.A.F. Twenty-six, childless and tenderhearted, she lavished on the young pilots of East Malford all her unfulfilled maternal warmth; and the rich peasant sensuality that was bred in her by generations of forebears who had worked on the land and never took a maid to the altar before they had put her fertility to the proof.

She worked in the Officers' Mess and her first daily concern was to ensure that the pilots at their dispersal points were well fed. In these hectic times lunch was eaten, on most days, on the airfield. Connie delivered the meals personally.

The Officers' Mess steward, who had seen service in the houses of the rich, and ran the mess in a manner which would not have disgraced them, approved of Cpl. Gates. If he was aware of the generous lengths to which she went in her elected role of comforter to the pilots, he maintained a perfect discretion.

They were discussing the lunch arrangements when the quietness of the mess was tom apart by the bellow of twelve Hurricanes directly overhead. Before the noise had died another squadron screamed over the roof, also on a southerly course.

The elderly man and the young woman looked at each other. He shook his head in an expression of bleak resignation. She flushed and glanced down at the sheet of paper in her hand, tears threatening. They shared an angry, impotent reaction: the number of lunches they were preparing was based on an illusion., From the list the mess secretary's office had given them, they knew that there were sixty-four pilots and nine intelligence and technical officers out at dispersals. Of the pilots, eighteen were N.C.O.s, but the mess steward had arranged with the Sergeants' Mess caterer that he would send food out for them also and take repayment in rations. Sixty-four flying men to feed, then; in theory. Both knew that, by lunch time, there would not be so many.

Soon after "A" Flight had come back from their first sortie, "B" Flight were scrambled. But the order came too late and they returned, frustrated, without having made contact with the enemy. While they were climbing to get above the top layer of Me. 109s, and up-sun, the raiders turned south and made back for France. Vapour trails patterned the sky and there were drifting plumes and patches of smoke from burning aircraft. In the distance the sun glinted on the fast-disappearing Heinkels and their escorting Messerschmitts.

The disgruntled pilots of "B" Flight flung themselves into their chairs and cursed the slow reactions of their seniors in the various Operations Rooms all the way up to Headquarters Fighter

Command itself. They swore and grumbled because they had no proper idea of the problems that their commanders at Group and Command Headquarters had to grapple with. For the men who flew the Hurricanes and Spitfires it was simply a matter of attack and defence. The enemy approached, the radiolocation (radar) early warning system alerted the Operations Rooms, and all that the Group Commanders and controllers had to do was send fighters off at once, giving them time to make height and position themselves up-sun. Then, despite the Me 109s' greater speed and rate of climb, they would reach the bombers before the enemy fighters could intervene. In their minds, it was all very straightforward and easy.

The pilots, knowing only the system of defence and little of its defects or the scarcity of aircraft in Fighter Command, and with no personal experience of controlling, over-simplified. To them it seemed plain that two squadrons could keep a hundred German fighters busy while a third shot down the bombers. If there was an early warning system, and if fighter squadrons were kept at readiness all day, what prevented the top brass from ordering them off in time to do just that?

But the situation and the tactics were not, in reality, so uncomplicated, and the pity of it was that nobody explained to the fighting airmen how the defence system really operated. Spoof raids would appear on the radar screens to draw up the British fighters; then landed, and while the R.A.F. was refuelling the real raids came in. So someone in command had to decide whether each enemy movement was a feint or genuine. Early radar was inaccurate. Electrical faults were frequent. Someone had to decide how to make the best use of the seven hundred fighters and fourteen hundred fighter pilots the R.A.F. had, against a Luftwaffe that could call on nearly fifteen hundred bombers and over a thousand fighters: and it was the bombers which would obliterate Britain's factories, airfields and towns; the fighters could only knock out the defending fighters. And their pilots.

172 Squadron amused itself in its various ways.

"Catch!" Massey flung aside the magazine he was trying to read and grabbed successfully for the hurled orange that was sailing towards him; only he didn't notice that there were two of them, and the second one biffed him between the eyes, making him yell and demand arbitration.

Sqdn. Leader Maxwell, disturbed in his reading of intelligence reports clipped to a plywood board, glanced around. His sensitive bony face gave him an austere look: a good instrument of discipline. In fact, he was a tolerant man; except towards Germans. The Squadron Medical Officer was sitting comfortably on his motor cycle, propped on its stand, chatting to two of the sergeant pilots and Bernie Harmon. Maxwell let his eyes dwell for a while on Pilot Officer Harmon. He knew he worried too much about Bernie, but after all who wouldn't worry about a twenty-year-old brat who looked seventeen and had shot down eleven hostiles already, with five probables and a dozen or so badly damaged; who had won a D.F.M. and whom he had recently recommended for a D.F.C. The boy looked too frail to fire a popgun, let alone eight .303 Brownings, yet he fed on Germans with the appetite of an ogre.

Bernie Harmon had entered the R.A.F. Apprentices' School at the age of fourteen and qualified as a sergeant pilot four years later. It was only two months since he had been commissioned.

Maxwell and the M.O. watched him with covert anxiety for signs of a mental or physical breakdown, but they might as well have expected a crack in the Rock of Gibraltar. Harmon was a Cockney from Bethnal Green, half-Jewish, sallow and stunted, brave as *a* lion. And now, for God's sake, Maxwell reflected irritably, the silly little sod had gone clean off his rocker as soon as he got his commission, and leaped into matrimony. Sarah, his brand new wife, small, dark, glowing, a full-blooded Jewess, was installed in lodgings in the local village. She and Bernie had bicycles, which they rode with perfect equilibrium after even the wildest squadron party: both of them being virtually teetotal. Maxwell felt that he had enough on his hands without a child bride (Sarah was eighteen) who might at any moment become a child widow. At the back of his mind, too, was a vague but discouraging notion that if Bernie did get the chop there would be a mournful visitation by a weeping rabbi, all long black coat, greasy ringlets and beard, and biblical incantations; not to mention a tear bottle.

If only Bernie Harmon were a bit more like Sergeant Wilkins, now. Wilkie was a burly, laconic Geordie who had fled the coal-mines to breathe clean air as a regular airman. He shared with his flight commander, Flt. Lt Poynter, a passionate love for cars. There he was now, pottering with the engine of his red "J" model M.G. while Spike Poynter hovered around with his head also under the bonnet. Spike's own elderly Aston Martin (bought before the war with a small legacy), a draughty noisy 1½ litre open sports job with a polished aluminium body, stood in the shade of a Nissen hut. Other members of the squadron often told its devoted owner that it was a totally useless form of transport, because there was no room to stretch out with a bit of crumpet. This calumny always got a rise out of him. Cars were meant for one sort of fun and beds for quite another, and neither should be made to perform the other's function, he said. Nobody agreed with him, except Sergeant Wilkins: and even Wilkins, Maxwell suspected, would tell his superior officer, any minute now, to buzz off and tune his own motor. No need to worry about Wilkins; he was as solid and unflappable as they come.

Maxwell considered the two new arrivals, Cunningham and Webb: they sat a little apart from the rest, sharing a set of aircraft recognition cards; silhouettes of friendly and enemy aeroplanes depicted from various angles. They kept their distance not only because they sought quiet for their concentration but also because they felt diffident about mixing with the rest of the squadron. They were questioning each other seriously, each briefly holding a card up and asking what aircraft it shewed. Well, Maxwell told himself, that was one way to buy some insurance in staying alive; and avoid the ultimate crime of shooting down one of your own side. He had to approve, although these two new boys were more subdued than he liked his young officers to be. They had better lose their shyness soon: some of the pilots with twenty or thirty sorties to their names had only been with the squadron two or three weeks; there was no need to stand in awe of them.

Webb and Cunningham had arrived two days before from the same operational training unit, with only ten hours apiece on Hurricanes. Maxwell had not made them operational yet; had not dared to: first, the squadron would have to teach them how to fly a fighter in battle. The O.T.U.s merely gave them the rudiments: just enough to get them killed quickly. But there were no aircraft to spare for teaching these youngsters dog-fighting. At the present casualty rate, pilots were being turned out of training schools before they were ready for action; and they were the ones who got killed, while the veterans survived.

He had no way of knowing that, a month later, pilots would leave some of the training units without ever having fired their guns, even at a towed target.

Despite the lack of experienced pilots and serviceable aircraft, he had to find some way of giving these new types adequate instruction. If he had been praised for his concern he would have replied, with unconvincing but statutory cynicism, that he had enough letters of condolence to write every week as it was without adding unnecessarily to the number.

He knew that the risks were the same for all of them but felt particular compassion for new arrivals; especially these, with their pink-faced schoolboy youthfulness. At their age he had just entered the Royal Air Force College at Cranwell and started learning to fly comparatively slow and easily handled biplanes. Whereas today's new pilots, who were not even professionals but war-time temporaries, were being rushed through their training and into the cockpits of fast, sensitive Hurricanes and Spitfires; and thrown into action at once, before they had learned to shoot decently or fly with polish.

The telephone rang on his desk: two Hurricanes were already being brought over from the hangar and the third would be serviceable in an hour; well ahead of schedule. Maxwell congratulated his Engineer Officer: he, and the technical flight sergeant and the rest of the ground crews, all deserved medals, he thought, for their hard and skilful work.

The telephone rang again and a few seconds later twelve pilots were pelting for their aircraft.

Five or six were left staring after them and there were a couple of absentees; even at the height of war, ordinary human affairs took their toll: one was having dental treatment at that moment and another was on leave to visit a dying mother.

Pilot Officer Cunningham turned to P.O. Webb and said "That's the twelfth scramble we've watched in forty-eight hours. At that rate, with aircraft coming back badly damaged, or not at all, we'll see another dozen and still not be operational."

"Might as well go back to O.T.U. At least they did have some aircraft for us."

They had jumped to their feet when the scramble order was given and watched the Hurricanes waddling and bouncing over the airfield, gaining flying speed and soaring away beyond the boundary fence.

Nigel Cunningham glanced at his friend. "Makes me feel such a fraud to sit here doing damn-all, when my poor bloody parents are worried sick imagining I'm fighting battles all day."

"Hadn't thought of that Know how you feel. Wish you hadn't brought it up, though: feeling frustrated is bad enough without feeling bloody bogus into the bargain. Come on, let's get on with these silhouettes."

They put their heads together and sat with their shoulders touching, subconsciously drawing mutual comfort from one another, as they became absorbed again in their study.

Pierre Dunal watched them from behind his sun glasses, speculating. He had been feeling sorry for them ever since their arrival, as he did for all newcomers to the close, guarded fraternity of the squadron. He knew they were only nineteen. He was only three years older than they, but the gap between a sophisticated Frenchman of good family and callow British youths was ineffable. He very much wanted to bridge it and offer them some open sympathy, but it was not for him to make the move when their own compatriots ignored them. He knew that this was neither from unfriendliness nor from any convention that pilots had to prove themselves in action before being truly accepted, but from sheer preoccupation and weariness. And, in some, a deliberate avoidance of close friendships which were quickly and hurtfully ended by death. It was not good to care too much about one's comrades in these times; better to take their loss without any personal sense of bereavement.

There were many reasons why newcomers to any fighter squadron this long, brilliant summer met an indifferent welcome.

Dunal's eyes lingered sympathetically just the same, as the two friends sat in such manifest intimacy. He hoped the *voyou*, the *grosse brute* Blakeney-Smith would not take it into his head to molest them with his acid taunts. After all, their unconscious yearning for mutual comfort and affection among strange surroundings was no more unnatural than his own for *la belle* Connie; or Blakeney-Smith's for the barmaids and chorus girls whom his money bought.

Beyond the Airmen's Married Quarters was a pasture shielded from the camp by trees. Here was privacy for the taking of illicit photographs. Tuttle took first turn at wearing Flying Officer Knight's best tunic.

He stood in the sunlight, smiling; broad-shouldered and bare headed, his thick black hair set in an unfortunate quiff which would not have been approved in an Officers' Mess, even in wartime. He smoothed the last wrinkle out of the officer's tunic and presented his left side to the photographer. For a moment his thick fingers went up to run over the embroidered wings on the breast; the badge stood proud of the cloth and was silkily smooth: it had taken Knight more than a year's hard work and no small measure of guts to earn the right to wear it.

"Take yer toime," the batman admonished his friend with the camera. "Yer know 'ow 'ard it is to get fillums, so down't wiste it. There's a war on y'know."

Hafner had been granted his wish. Yet another force of bombers, forty of them, had been sent to attack R.A.F. airfields in southern England. Nearly a hundred Me. 109s and Me. 110s escorted them. II JG 97 flew high cover, which would give them the chance to attack the Spitfires and Hurricanes as soon as they appeared.

Private Greiner had swept and dusted Richter's room, tidied away his letters and the newspapers from home, and polished his boots and shoes. Now he was going to press Richter's spare uniforms and then he thought he would take a rest in the shade of a tree by the barn, where he would enjoy a pipe and read the

German newspapers: one of his own and one which he would borrow from his officer's room. It would never have occurred to him to pry into Hafner's mail, but borrowing his newspaper was a liberty he did allow himself: like his comrades, he craved news from home.

Greiner had no iron of his own, but the farmer's widow would lend him one. He had made a point of being civil to her. She had a hard enough job in running the farm since her husband was killed behind his field gun in the French retreat. Any German soldier who helped to lighten it could, maybe, expect some favours; she was a fine woman, broad bosomed and full lipped; and Greiner's wife was five hundred miles away.

For the use of her fiat iron he protected her from the marauding troops who came to pester her for eggs, milk and chickens. He thought he was already beginning to see signs of a thaw in her frosty demeanour towards the invaders who had widowed her. After all, he, a batman in the airforce, had had no hand in her bereavement. Why should she bear him a grudge? He was a decent, home-loving fellow, as no doubt her husband had been; and doubtless with the same burning desire to return to the plump arms of his wife. A little persistence and he was sure that Madame Prudhomme's legs, as well as her arms, would open to him.

He looked forward to an industrious morning and afternoon, with a well merited spell of leisure when his work was done; culminating in a little erotic Franco-German sodality sooner or later.

He did not ask much for himself. His first concern was to do his duty to Leutnant Hafner. If, in the course of it, he could get to lay his hand on the bare white leg of the farmer's widow, thick though it was, patterned with incipient varicose veins and more than a little hirsute, he was sure his master would not begrudge him the legitimate spoils of war. For the young devil was hot blooded enough himself.

He wholeheartedly admired and respected his officers. Some of the old soldiers on the Staffel affected to despise or ridicule them, and perhaps it was not pretence, maybe many of them did look on the officers as over-privileged and selfish, fair game for exploitation. Not that it was easy to exploit a German officer: the tough N.C.O.s made sure of that.

Greiner believed that "the Comrades", as the pilots called each other, were heroes. He could not imagine himself attempting the desperate deeds which were the fabric of their daily lives. If it would have relieved Hafner's nervous tension, on the bad days, to strike him, Greiner would willingly have stood to attention while he did so as often as he wished.

With a screech of wind noise and a roar of engines twelve aircraft of No. 1 Staffel climbed above the farm and spiralled out of sight to join the other twenty-four Messerschmitts of the Gruppe.

Greiner, with his square head tilted back, watched them. He hoped that the Virgin whose image on a disc of cheap white metal Hafner carried in his pocket would protect him. Being a Lutheran himself, he was sceptical about this.

SQUADRON LEADER MAXWELL LED HIS SQUADRON
in loose formation on their third sortie of the day, climbing north-eastward to make enough height to be above the enemy when they crossed the coast. Coming from the south, the Germans had the sun behind them: that was a disadvantage that the defenders could not completely offset, but they could at least intercept from abeam, either east or west, and avoid looking directly into the sun.

Maxwell's policy was to train all his pilots in leadership, although this sometimes meant leaving a good, battle-hardened – man behind so that a comparative novice could learn a new role.

It was something of a luxury in these hard pressed days, but Maxwell knew the importance of ensuring that every section, flight or squadron leader could be adequately replaced immediately. Neither he nor his flight commanders could be any more certain than the other pilots that they would return from a sortie. He was satisfied that either Lee or Poynter could take over his job; Knight, Harmon and one or two others could replace them; except that Harmon, as a very newly commissioned officer, was too junior and would have to jump a rank to get command of a flight.

Blakeney-Smith, in theory, should be ready for promotion. He was a regular officer with enough seniority. But it would have been an unhappy flight that Simple Simon commanded.

Jumper Lee was not satisfied with Blakeney-Smith's recent performance, Maxwell knew. Simon should not have let himself be separated from Dunal on the first sortie that morning: it was only the Frenchman's second chance at flying Number Two, and his experienced Number Three should have stayed as close to him as a destraining bailiff. But Jumper had taken immediate steps to ensure it didn't happen again.

Maxwell knew who would give the first warning call: Simon Blakeney-Smith, with his innate competitiveness, always determined to get in before anyone else. And the first accurate sighting would be given by Bernie Harmon. It was Bernie's sharpness of eye which was the basic reason for his longevity (barely twenty years of age but survivor of a hundred combats) and his lethal record of success in battle. With his superlative sense of timing, he acted at precisely the right split second: whether it was to turn, to dive, to climb or to shoot. With his abnormal vision he saw trouble coming soon enough to have made himself a legend for his brilliant evasive action.

Maxwell never knew whether to be amused or pitying when Blakeney-Smith legged it for his Hurricane on a scramble. Driven by the compulsion to outshine everyone, he was always first into the cockpit: he took care to sit on the fringe of the group outside the crew room door, or nearest the door when they sat inside, so as to be the closest to the dispersal line. On his long legs he lolloped across the grass like an absconding cashier. He boasted that although he never played games, and smoked, drank, and wenched more than anyone else on the squadron (he didn't: Jumper, and others, beat him at the last two and Pierre and Lottie smoked like overtime factory chimneys), he could outstrip them all when it came to a scramble.

"You've got damn-all to shew for it," Peter Knight told him one day. "You may get in your cockpit before the rest of us, but you don't seem to shoot down many hostiles." Even that direct rudeness did not deter Blakeney-Smith from reiterating the boast.

The C.O. had overheard his pilots, last week, discussing this vanity (among many) of the unlovable Simon's. They had thought it would be a good idea to persuade the adjutant to arrange a posting to 172 Squadron for any champion sprinter who happened to be leaving an operational training unit. They reckoned that Simple Simon would have apoplexy in his efforts to beat a trained athlete who could easily run a hundred yards in ten seconds. But Blakeney-Smith was not an interesting enough subject to hold their attention for long and the idea was dropped after half a day.

A minute later the radio crackled: "Yellow Leader from Yellow Two. Bandits ten-o'clock high." Blakeney-Smith on the ball.

His section leader sounded bored. "Spots before the eyes. Red Leader from Yellow One: about twenty one-o-nines one-o'clock, below."

Maxwell looked down to his right, then called Harmon: "Green Leader, see anything?"

"Twenty-four one-o-nines, at one o'clock, about twenty thousand. Bombers behind them at ten thousand."

Maxwell rocked his wings to get a better view. "I've got 'em. Blue and Green watch for fighters above. Red and Yellow, let's go for the bombers. Tallyho!"

Anne Holt stood on the lawn in front of her parents' house and scanned the sky.

She had been listening to gunfire. High overhead, machine guns rattled and occasionally she saw the sparkle of tracer. Nearby, light anti-aircraft guns pumped shells at the German bombers and then fell silent as the Gun Operations Room ordered them to cease fire for the safety of friendly fighters in the zone. Anne knew nothing about Gun Operations Room or the danger to the Spitfires and Hurricanes from friendly antiaircraft fire, and felt indignant because the Army was apparently leaving all the fighting to the R.A.F. Vapour trails streaked the whole area of sky that she could see.

The sights and sounds were familiar. She had seen many aeroplanes falling to the ground during the last few weeks. She had heard them explode and watched the smoke billow where men had died. She had seen parachutes open and drift earthward, each with a small human speck beneath it, often swinging like a pendulum.

She was a frequent guest at dances and cocktail parties in the Officers' Mess at East Malford and felt personally involved in the battles that she witnessed almost every day.

The first pilot who had taken her out was killed during the second week of their friendship. The next, who had survived long enough to escort her for a month, was now in hospital bumscarred and blinded in one eye. She was glad she had been kind to him; he wouldn't find it so easy to get girls when he came out of hospital with half his nose gone, disfigured cheeks and an empty eye socket.

And now there was Peter Knight and she was scared for him.

He wasn't as handsome as Charles (as Charles had been before enemy gunfire ripped his face to ruin), or as tall and magnificent as Pip, who was still strapped into his Hurricane at the bottom of the English Channel. But he had a straight look, mischievous eyes and good manners; he flirted mildly with her mother, who enjoyed it, and talked sport with her father, who took him seriously because he played rugger for Fighter Command.

She had gone out once with Blakeney-Smith. He had offered to take her to dinner after a mess party and she accepted because she was still grieving over Pip; and because she recognised some destructive sense of insecurity in Simon and pitied him. She did not enjoy herself. He tried to give the impression that anything different from his own way of doing things was either bad form, poor quality or old hat. He always knew how to fare better than the common herd: where the food was superior, which road was quickest, who dealt in black market supplies.

Recently he had taken to flaunting a complaisant A.T.S. officer who was ten years older than he and talked shrilly about her husband, a major who had been captured at Dunkirk. It was the fact that he was a senior officer, not that he was in a German prisoner of war camp, which prompted her to speak of him. Anne agreed with Peter and his friends that Simon's woman's husband had got the better of the bargain: he was free of her for a year or two; with little incentive to risk escape.

Anne went indoors. As long as she stayed outside she watched the sky compulsively for a tumbling Hurricane or Spitfire at the end of a lengthening trail of smoke.

She found her mother in the kitchen with the cook, making jam. She lingered to help absent-mindedly for a while, but as soon as she heard fighters returning to the airfield two miles away she hurried to a window to count them. She had seen twelve leave. She did not want to know how many did not return, yet she was overcome by the compulsion to find out just that. She leaned on the window sill and felt her hands trembling.

Cpl. Gates sat beside the driver of a pick-up van which was on its way around the perimeter road. The back was laden with trays full of sandwiches and fruit and urns of tea and coffee.

172 and 82 Squadrons had been scrambled an hour ago and by now all those who were coming back would have landed. 699 had gone back to their messes, released for an hour. The officer pilots had been in high spirits and Connie had heard them tell

an off-duty controller that the squadron was officially operational from two-o'clock. They would be back at their dispersal, Mae Wests on and ready to scramble, half an hour before then.

It was a situation with which Connie was familiar and she knew how they would be feeling about being operational this time tomorrow. The squadron they had replaced had spent only six weeks at East Malford. They too had flown in jubilantly and whooped with joy when they were made operational two days after their arrival. Of the nineteen pilots who had come to East Malford, only seven flew out alive and unhurt.

It wrung her heart out to see the faces of these eager young men grow thin and lined with fatigue, grey with fear and tension: and she knew what must be in store for the confident 699.

The van stopped first at 172's dispersal area. Every head turned: not because the pilots' hunger pangs prompted them, but because they knew what they were about to see and didn't want to miss any of it.

Connie knew why they were looking, and she aimed to please. Taking her time, she opened the door slowly and first put one of the two sexiest legs at East Malford out of the door, and then the other. For a carefully arranged few seconds her skirt rode well above her knees and she pointed the toes of her brilliantly polished shoes daintily, as though feeling for the ground. In defiance of regulations she wore silk stockings; but they were the official grey and none of the W.A.A.F. officers felt like chiding an N.C.O. Besides, they wore the same kind themselves.

More than one of the officer and sergeant pilots had shewn their appreciation of Cpl. Gates's kindness by giving her clothing coupons, obtained by diverse means. They felt privileged, as they watched those graceful legs emerge to public view, that they knew what the unexposed portions looked like as well. It was a tribute to Connie's discretion that none of those who had received her favours knew with which of his comrades he shared them.

Pierre Dunal paused in the act of lighting his twentieth cigarette of the day and peered through the flame of his lighter with a reminiscent gleam in his eye. If it hadn't been for Connie's solicitude when he got news that his sixteen-year-old brother had been shot by the Germans and his sister and mother raped, he would have disintegrated. As it was, he nearly crashed twice and barely missed being shot down a dozen times, he was flying so raggedly, before Connie's perceptiveness led her to provide the right therapy.

Flight Sergeant Viccar, the redoubtable Bishop, who had just shot down his fifth enemy aircraft and was bursting to tell someone about it, grinned at her; a flash of reminiscent thought about a night not long ago, when he was close to nervous collapse, took his mind off his kill while he admired her figure. In shirt sleeves on this hot summer's day she shewed off her bosom to great advantage behind the tightly strained, thin material. He had been allowed to see it unconcealed, when Connie cured him of his nervous tension with her understanding ministrations.

Jumper Lee, loosening the paisley silk scarf he always wore, smiled appreciatively at this delectable bit of bogle: he felt sure the game was on, there, if he wanted to play, but he hadn't yet descended to having to sleep with the domestic staff; and anyway it was bad for discipline for flight lieutenants to foul their own doorsteps. But he could, and did, look at the goods even if he couldn't maul 'em.

Peter Knight, wearing a club-striped silk square in place of a collar and tie, compared Connie with Anne Holt and decided there wasn't much in it; a compliment to Anne. He liked Cpl. Gates's soft west country burr: it was a pity she couldn't call him "M'dear-r-r", but her "Sir-r-r" was a joy to the ear; and the rest of her didn't exactly hurt the eye, he conceded. He looked with amusement towards Massey.

Six-gun almost slavered over Connie Gates. She was self-possessed and friendly, and he seemed to make so much time with her that he could never understand why she wouldn't date him. It wasn't easy to date a girl who worked in the mess; the squadron usually went about in a bunch and it wouldn't have been tactful to take her to a party with the C.O. and his wife and some of the others. But he had asked her to take in a movie and have dinner on one of his rare off-duty days, and she had refused. Goddamit, he grumbled inwardly as he admired her now, what was the matter with him? He usually scored when he wanted to.

But Connie's friendly rejection of his advances was due to the fact that there was *nothing* the matter with Six-gun Massey, He was mentally, as well as physically, tough enough to cope with the stresses of air fighting; he gave no signs of being in danger of a breakdown. He needed no help and Connie's generosity was essentially a matter of succour. As long as there were lame ducks whom she could comfort and cure, the hawks like Massey won no response from her.

When she and the driver had, with the help of some of the aircraftmen, unloaded enough trays, she climbed back into the van. Nobody thought of eating until the last flutter of lace and the last promising inch of long, silk-clad leg had disappeared from sight.

"On going in to attack I selected a Heinkel 111 on the extreme left of the eight leading bombers. I attacked from the starboard quarter and opened fire at three hundred yards aiming at the front of the e/a (enemy aircraft). I saw strikes at the starboard wing root and in the cockpit. On diving past the e/a I looped, half-rolled off the top and attacked again from the port beam, shooting into the cockpit. I evidently killed the pilot, as the Heinkel went into a steep dive from which it did not recover. I later saw it crash in the Channel after two of the crew had baled out.

"Before seeing it hit the sea, I had begun my attack on the aircraft behind it, coming in again from the port beam, but had to break off after two seconds to avoid collision with another Hurricane.

"At this point, the controller informed us that another squadron had been scrambled to deal with the bombers and we were to intercept the high cover enemy fighters.

"Red One ordered us to formate on him at fifteen thousand, at which point Yellow Two said he had been hit and was baling out. As we had been making individual attacks, I did not know where he was. I saw a Hurricane going down on my port side and the pilot bale out. There appeared to be no smoke or flame and I presumed that the engine had been put out of action.

"Yellow Three and I joined Red Section and found the rest of the squadron in action at twenty-five thousand feet. I attacked the leader of a formation of four Me. 109s from head-on, after which I broke upwards to port and had a dogfight Yellow Three stayed with me and we scored hits on two 109s, of which one broke off with oil and smoke coming from it."

Flying Officer Knight read over his combat report and said "We turned inside them but they outnumbered us, and while Six-gun was covering my tail two of them were getting on his. With a complete section, if Yellow Two had stayed with us, we'd have got at least two of them."

Herrick pushed a sheet of paper towards Pilot Officer Massey. "Want to add anything, Six-gun?"

The American took his own report without a word, and scanned it.

"I attacked the Heinkel second from the end of the leading line, giving it a short burst in the starboard engine before breaking away to come in again from astern. I silenced the rear gunner, then fired a long burst into the starboard engine, which stopped. I then dived past and came up from slightly below, shooting at the port engine, which caught fire. The e/a lost height rapidly. I saw two survivors bale out.

"I then rejoined Yellow Leader and we formed up with Red Flight to intercept some 109s. We had a dogfight and damaged two.

"Yellow Two passed the Heinkel I first attacked, and I saw him climb away to starboard. I later saw a Hurricane attack a Heinkel on the outside of the formation, from high on its quarter, and thought it must be Yellow Two. I also saw a pilot bale out of a Hurricane which was in an inverted spin but not on fire."

Both pilots rejoined the rest of the squadron around the trestle table on which their lunch had been laid, leaving Herrick with his paperwork, struggling to sort a clear and accurate account of the engagement from the often involved and conflicting combat reports. It was as well that he was a newspaper reporter in civilian life.

Bernie Harmon was the centre of a gesticulating, noisy argument. His sharp little black eyes snapped with gaiety as he relived the battle in which he had neatly picked off a Me. 109 before Spike Poynter, who was flying well ahead of him and had chosen it as his target, could open fire.

Spike said aggrievedly, "You can't expect us all to be ruddy Daniel Boones, Bernie: you might have left that one to me; I had him cold. *You* could easily have got another!"

"How was I to know which one you were going to attack!"

"And you frightened hell out of me when your tracer came whizzing over my head from astern: I thought I'd been jumped."

Knight and Massey joined in the laughter.

The squadron had done well Only Blakeney-Smith had been shot down; and he was seen to bale out safely. Three Hurricanes had suffered minor damage. And that was all. In return, they had destroyed six Heinkels and damaged four. Harmon and Lotnikski had each destroyed a Me. 109 and the whole squadron had, between them, severely damaged three or four more.

Maxwell went into his office to telephone 82's commander. They had been in the same year at the Royal Air Force College and the two squadrons worked closely. He came out looking pleased: 82 had all come back, except for two pilots who had forced-landed. They had shot down four 109s.

"If the bastards aren't too ambitious this afternoon we should stand down in time for a good party tonight," Maxwell had just observed, when the Ops Room telephone in the crew room interrupted him.

Hands that were in the act of raising sandwiches to hungry mouths either fell limply or thrust the food quickly between champing teeth. Cups of coffee were drained or set aside.

Nigel Cunningham and his friend Webb looked into each other's apprehensive eyes and, without a word, both walked quickly behind the nearer hut and retched. F/Sgt Viccar's hand began to tremble so violently that he spilled his coffee. Dunal gave a convulsive jerk that sent his cigarette spinning through the air, to be pounced on immediately by Moonshine with an appreciative bark.

They all listened to the voice of the airman who was taking the message from Operations. It seemed to be a longer one than the usual scramble order. And when the telephone orderly came to the door it wasn't in his habitual rush. He was grinning. He walked over to Sqdn. Ldr. Maxwell.

"Message from the controller, sir. Flying Officer Blakeney-Smith was picked up by an air-sea rescue launch. He's unhurt, sir. The controller says he'll be back on the station in a couple of hours."

Nobody cheered; as they might have if the good news had been about any of the others.

Dunal remarked: "Now he will exhaust himself trying to arrange an airlift; but in a Blenheim, of course, to go one better than me."

When attacking bombers which outnumbered them, particularly when there was no close escort, fighters did not necessarily attack in formation, with each section following its leader. Knight could not criticise his Number Two for peeling off and selecting his own target when the C.O. had ordered individual attacks. But there was something else to discuss. He drew Massey aside and spoke in an undertone.

"Did you see Simon after we broke?"

"Nope. And I'm only assuming he was the guy I saw coming in for a high quarter attack."

"So you didn't see him hit?"

"He wasn't hit, Pete." Massey was full of scorn. "He was having a go because there were no 109s in shooting distance. But as soon as the Boss called us off to go after the high cover, Blakeney-Smith quit. That's what I reckon, anyways. He's no eager beaver."

With compressed lips, Knight walked away angrily without another word.

But Six-gun called after him: "And I'll tell you something else. Pierre's wrong. He won't hitch a ride in an airplane; that would get him back in time for the next scramble, maybe. And Simple Goddam Simon don't like a-flyin'. So he'll take his time. We won't see him before stand-down."

Knight felt his ears burning with vicarious shame and stiffened his back in embarrassed anger as he kept walking away from his American friend; who, he knew, was speaking the bitter truth about a British comrade; to whom Knight was bound by every sort of loyalty.

Pie went into the crew room and picked up the second telephone to ask for Anne's number. It was against regulations to use it for private calls, but Knight, after an all-ranks dance once, had given one of the telephone operators a pleasant hour in the back of his car, and she and her colleagues lived in hopes of getting more; so they bent the rules for any officer calling from dispersals.

Talking to Anne was the distraction and catharsis he needed at that moment. The bell had rang only twice when she answered breathlessly. She gasped with relief when she heard his voice. He invited her to dinner at the Spider's Web: his father had sent him a five-pound note the previous day.

"See you at half-past seven," he said, and strolled back to his friends, his dog jumping playfully at his side. He bent down and fondled its head. There were still some sandwiches left and he shared one with Moonshine.

Lee was shifting impatiently from leg to leg. He kept looking at the clear sky. Knight, guessing what was coming, watched him go and speak to the C.O. and then return.

"If you've finished wolfing, Pete, we'll take the two new boys up and see how much they know. We've got three replacement aircraft coming in this afternoon."

"And more new boys?"

"No, the A.T.A. are ferrying these in. Two of them are going back in that Magister that got stranded here the other day. The third one's staying: in the W.A.A.F. officers' quarters," he added with a grin.

"At last! I've always wanted to get a close-up of one of these Air Transport Auxiliary women pilots." Massey, who had overheard, looked animated.

"Bet you can't get a date with her tonight/ Knight challenged instantly.

"How much you wanna bet?"

"Dinner at the Spider's Web."

"You've got yourself a deal, Pete." Six-gun put his hand to his forehead in pretended agony. "Hold it! What am I saying? Suppose she has a face like a coyote's ass?"

"Then you're bound to win your bet: the plain ones are always the most grateful."

"Who looks at the mantelpiece when he's poking the fire?" asked Jumper. "Come on, Pete, let's get airborne." He beckoned to the two nineteen-year-olds who were hovering on the outskirts of everything, keeping their own counsel but watching, listening with a mixture of eagerness and apprehension. "Cunningham, take "A". You and I are going to do some dogfighting. Webb, yours is "N": Peter Knight's going to shew you the ropes. Come on, pull finger, let's get cracking."

The two youngsters were galvanised. In an instant they cast aside their distress and dashed cheerfully into the crew room for their parachutes, helmets and Mae Wests.

Knight, walking beside one of them, asked pleasantly: "You're Nigel, aren't you?"

"No, sir. Roderick… Roddy."

"O.K. Roddy. I'm Peter. Only call the Boss "Sir". Don't they teach you anything at training schools these days?"

"They don't teach us much about dogfighting." He had just the right note of ruefulness. Knight approved of his answer.

He looked quickly at the boy and grinned encouragingly. "Good for you, Roddy. I don't know a hell of a lot about it, either. Don't let it worry you. This isn't going to be a high-dive-into-no-water effort: I'll explain what I want you to do and give you plenty of time."

Webb was grateful for the sense of security and the reassurance that Knight's friendly, off-hand words gave him. He could imagine how different a briefing he would have received from Blakeney-Smith, whose every sentence implied that he was in the ultimate know about everything and determined to take unfair advantage of you. Knight was not much older than himself, but at once imparted confidence and encouragement. Even his blunt-featured, cheer-fully pugnacious face and thick, disorderly fair hair were part of it.

Knight's rigger scrambled down from the port wing of "E", holding two cans of paint. A sixth white and black German cross gleamed, wet and new, on the fuselage.

"You don't waste much time, do you?" Knight assumed a false scowl.

"The more of these they sees, the more them Jerries'll leave you alone, sir: scares 'em off when they see 'ow many you've shot down."

"I wish I had your confidence."

Knight, dogfighting with the callow Webb, thought seriously for the first time about the vulnerability of new pilots like this. He had always supposed that the longer a man was on front-line service, the worse his prospects of survival.

At the outbreak of the war he had, like most regulars, taken it for granted that he would more probably be killed than survive. The thought had not frightened or depressed him: although it was so personal, he remained objective about it. It was impossible to imagine being dead. In the early days he had had disagreeable thoughts about *how* he might be killed: being shot in the guts, burned, or trapped in a diving Hurricane would be hideous; what happened finally was something everyone had to face eventually, and of itself it did not terrify him.

He supposed that young Webb must have had the same thoughts, so to encourage him he let himself be out-manoeuvred two or three times.

Then he began to think about Blakeney-Smith and instantly slid into such intense concentration on his flying that the unhappy Webb had no chance at all: and each time he had Webb in his sights he told himself that it was Blakeney-Smith's heraldically adorned Hurricane there, tempting a blast from his guns. He saw Blakeney-Smith's snouty, pudgy face with its silly moustache and had to blink to make himself realise that he was only playing a game; and that he was playing it with the pink-cheeked Webb whom he had decided to encourage.

So once again he allowed his pupil to bounce him from up-sun and gave him words of praise.

He thought how convenient it would have been if the Germans had picked Blakeney-Smith up and locked him away for the duration, where he could no longer irritate the rest of the squadron.

But suppose the oaf had turned up again, more obnoxious than ever after a successful prison break?

No, that was one thing they would never have to worry about: Simon Blakeney-Smith would make the most willing prisoner of war of all time.

IF NO ORDERS CAME WITHIN THE NEXT HOUR IT would be the end of the hard, sunlit working day. During the night the bombers would go out unescorted and the fighter Geschwader would be set free.

Oberleutnant Richter was at ease in a canvas chair, his feet propped on an ammunition box, turning the pages of a physical culture magazine. Erich Hafner and Otto Ihlefeld were seated nearby with girlie magazines open on their knees. Their comrades pressed around them and there was a continuous exchange of lewd comment, banter and laughter. The provocatively posed girls on the glossy pages excited the younger men's lust. But Richter had no one with whom to share his enjoyment of the oiled, muscular, superbly developed male physiques. He felt jealous of the others with their common interest so openly shared. If he gave way here to his own urge he would meet disaster, if he resisted it he would become neurotic. He had better go on leave for twenty-four hours: Paris or Lille would provide complaisant youths and the safety valve he so badly needed.

He put down the magazine abruptly, consulted his watch and stood up.

Instantly the group around Hafner and Ihlefeld stiffened and the seated officers began to rise.

Richter beckoned to a youngster who had been sitting by himself, too shy to join the group. "Come on, Keiling, let's see what you're made of."

The boy, who had already leaped to his feet, blushed and stammered. "S-s-sir?"

"Get in your aircraft, man. I'm going to take you up for a lesson in air combat."

"*Ja-wohl! Herr Oberleutnant. Sofort!*" He ran down the line of Messerschmitts. Since reporting to the Staffel the previous evening he had been waiting for someone to notice him; and now, at last, it was the godlike C.O. himself who had condescended to put him through his paces. He would have something worthwhile to write in his letter home tonight.

The rest of the pilots watched the two 109s take off, critically. When they were out of sight, Hafner asked "Who's coming into Boulogne for dinner?"

There was some groaning and slapping of empty pockets. Two or three agreed to go into town; others said they would join the party after dining in mess. Somebody suggested taking girls along with them, someone else thought it would be fun to tour the best brothels. They forgot the war as they cheerfully made their plans.

They were invaders, hated and resented. They had to make their own substitute for ordinary communal life; the townspeople would not accept them. They were cut off from normal genial intercourse with their fellow men. The billets they had requisitioned were German enclaves in an area from which most of the civilian inhabitants had been driven out. They were virtually living in a wasteland. A few French people were allowed to remain on the farms and in the villages but their movements were restricted. Those Germans who could visit the nearby towns were a fortunate minority and even they had to accept ostracism. They could eat in the restaurants, drink in the bars and cafés, buy presents to send home, frequent the brothels; but none of the French spoke willingly to them.

The officers took girls back to their quarters but sent them hurriedly away the next morning. Those women who sought the Germans' company did so because they accepted them as the new and permanent overlords of France; of Europe, indeed. They did so because, like young women the world over, they wanted to enjoy some gaiety; and the Germans offered abundant food and drink, boisterous parties, male adulation. The war was lost and the French would have to live in a new environment, so the sooner they learned to make the best of it the better. It was a specious but human philosophy. And besides, many of their new rulers were fine looking men; it was no hard-ship to accept their embraces. Conquerors have a special aura; the appeal of power and the glamour of valour and the force of arms. Not many women are proof against it, ultimately.

Nonetheless the evenings had an essential loneliness for young Erich Hafner and his friends, despite the easy availability of food, drink and pretty women.

Hafner punched his friend Ihlefeld on the shoulder. "You can have my blonde tonight, Otto. I fancy that redhead you've been keeping to yourself."

"All right. That'll suit everyone: I'm getting bored with the redhead, and the blonde has been making eyes at me behind your back for days…"

"You lying dog!"

Simon Blakeney-Smith knew all about fear; just as he knew all about bullying, for he had been to a Jesuit boarding school.

He had suffered especial cruelty at the hands of the Society of Jesus because he was ignorant of Catholic dogma when his parents first sent him to their expensive college. The Jesuits appeared to know only one way of teaching a boy anything: to thrash it into him with the ferrula, the brutal whalebone and rubber instrument with which they beat their pupil's hand. After two years he ran away, but his father forced him to return.

Blakeney-Smith had a morbid fear of eternal damnation, and it was this terror of hell which made him so reluctant a warrior.

While he was being driven back to East Malford in an ambulance he relived every detail of those horrifying moments of combat. He had felt his aircraft shudder as bullets hit; he didn't know where, or how much damage they had done. He had been quick-thinking enough to switch off his engine, roll his fighter on to its back and jump clear at once. He reasoned that it was most likely that he would have had to bale out anyway. He hadn't waited to find out whether his Hurricane was badly damaged; he had merely acted prudently.

He dragged himself away from his thoughts and gave his full attention to the pretty F.A.N.Y. who was driving the ambulance. She had been trying to encourage him to talk ever since they set off. He offered her a cigarette ("I hope you like Turks, what?"), lit a cheroot for himself ("Sure you don't mind the smell?"); and presently produced a leather-covered silver flask ("Useful in the hunting field, y'know") of whisky. "I always carry this in case I have to swim around a long time and get cold. I didn't touch it today: the A.S.R. boys were unusually quick."

She looked at him admiringly. "You've been through this before, then?"

"Well, one can't expect not to get a ducking now and then," he replied evasively. "Look, why don't you pull off the road and we'll have a drink."

That was the first of many stops.

Later, the pubs opened their back doors to them out of hours; in deference to the red cross, his pilot's wings and the story of rescue from the sea.

By the time they had emptied the flask and drunk more brandies at a "Red Lion", a "Marquis of Granby" and a "King's Head", the F.A.N.Y.'s inhibitions were banished.

As they drove away from the last pub. Simon put his hand on her knee, under her skirt and kissed her.

The ambulance swerved. In mock reproof, she said "Sir, I can't drive and smooch at the same time."

"Then park over there, behind those trees."

"Is that an order?"

"Yes. In the interests of road safety!"

"I'm not sure that an order like that doesn't constitute rape…"

"In that case…"

A stretcher was comfortable enough for what they urgently wanted to do.

The girl's lips were orange-pink and shiny. Her well tailored uniform stripped off with a provocative rustle of silken underwear. She turned her back to Blakeney-Smith: "Undo my bra, darling." There was a moment of impatient fumbling; she turned to face him again and encircled his neck with her arms, shivering and sighing.

A long time later she murmured "Are you sure no one can see us from the road?"

"Much too far."

"But just suppose someone does stop?"

"You're the First Aid Nursing Yeomanry, giving first aid."

"Oh, Sweetie, you think of everything!"

When eventually the ambulance dropped Flying Officer Blakeney-Smith at the Officers' Mess as the pilots of all three squadrons were coming off duty, several stopped with interest to see a dainty girl in trim uniform step nimbly out of the driving seat and give him a smart salute and a saucy smile. "Goodbye, sir. I hope I'll have the pleasure of driving you again some time. Soon."

For once, sophisticated Simon was lost for words.

It had not been such a hard day after all. Six-nine-nine were scrambled on their first operation early in the afternoon and promptly lost two pilots: one shot to death and the other entangled in his own parachute, which fouled the tail fin of his crippled Hurricane and dragged him down with it to make a hole in the ground from which it would take several hours' digging to entricate what was left of his body.

Eighty-two had been called on only twice. One-seven-two were scrambled at half-past four, but too late to make contact: once more they saw the enemy bombers well to the east of them, and by the time they were in position the German raiders had already attacked their targets and were on their way back. They were irritable but the disappointment did not lessen their elation over that morning's successes.

The arrival of the three replacement Hurricanes had caused a welcome diversion. The dark blue uniformed pilots of the Air Transport Auxiliary were an unfamiliar sight, for the organisation was still few in numbers. None of the East Malford pilots had ever seen a woman flying a fighter. They watched with critical interest as she came over the hedge and made a perfect landing: her head seemed to leave a lot of clearance below the canopy; she looked too small to handle a Hurricane.

"Now's your chance, Six-gun," prompted Knight.

The American grunted without enthusiasm. The three Hurricanes taxied over to 172's dispersal and there was a general movement as people stood up, stretched, pretended not to be curious, but somehow began drifting towards them.

The woman pilot took off her helmet and released an abundance of chestnut hair. Six-gun Massey whistled to himself and began to hurry. By the time she was ready to climb down from the port wing he was there with a hand outstretched to help her. This, he thought, was the time to take the utmost advantage of his foreignness, which he knew was a powerful attraction to British girls.

He came from Texas and could ham the part with devastating effect. "Howdy, Ma'am. Welcome to East Malford, on behalf of 172 Squadron. I'm Burt Massey, known to one and all as Six-gun." Might as well plunge right in; the competition was apt to get a little fierce around here: "I hope you'll join me and my buddies for a drink this evening. And maybe a bite to eat."

The girl, who was not more than five feet and one inch tall, had an attractive, freckled face. She paused in the act of climbing down and looked at him with twinkling eyes while he supported her with one large hand under her elbow. "Hi, Six-gun. I'm Elaine Dundry Todd, from Birmingham, Alabama. What part of li'l old Texas are you-all from?"

Massey let out a wild, cowboy whoop of delight. His evening was made.

There was one possible snag; the two surnames. The first would be her maiden name: who and where was husband Todd? What the hell! She looked like a lot of fun, anyways.

Squadron Leader Maxwell came forward and claimed her. His calm expression belied a mischievous glint in his eyes. "If you don't feel like eating in the mess, Mrs Todd, my wife and I would be delighted… we live very near." He took note, from the corner of his eye, of Six-gun's look of betrayal.

She gave him a dazzling smile and turned a mischievous one on Massey. "Thank you very much, Squadron Leader Maxwell, but I guess I already have a date."

The C.O.'s eyebrows shot up and he fixed a brief glare on Six-gun; muttered just audibly "Faster reaction than you ever shew in the air," which was unfair, and aloud: "I see. Well, that's fine. I'm sure you'll be well looked after. We'll meet during the evening, no doubt."

"I'll look forward to that. Thank you." He walked away with the other two ferry pilots, to put them in the car which would take them to the aircraft they were to fly back. She accepted a cigarette from one of her admirers and a cup of tea from another. Maxwell came back and offered to send her to the W.A.A.F. officers' quarters in his own staff car, but she declined charmingly. "If I'm not in the way, I'd love to stay right here for a while. I just adore the atmosphere of a squadron. I delivered a new Wellington to Scampton last week…" But that was as far as she was allowed to get before the heresy of mentioning bombers and a bomber station to a fighter squadron was interrupted by theatrical groans. "Oh, I get it. Pardon me. But of course "Hurricane" is a dirty word at Scampton."

"That," Massey told her, "is subversive propaganda."

She was still around when stand-down came. Spike Poynter drove her off in his Aston Martin to drop her at her billet before he set off to rejoin his wife in their flat in East Malford. He drove as though he were taking part in a race, although he had only three miles to go. He had been married for six months; a great deal sooner, as a regular officer, than he would have if there had not been a war. He still could not get used to his good fortune and had rapidly become the most uxorious husband on the station.

There was some argument about who should drive Blakeney-Smith's Bentley back to the mess. No one much wanted to, but they felt it would be mean to leave it at dispersals.

"Not me. I'm walking back with Moonshine." Knight left the group.

"Hell, I'll take it. Come on, you guys, climb aboard."

Massey took the wheel and several others piled in. "If Simon doesn't make it back this evening, darned if I won't borrow this jallopy to take that li'l old Alabama gal out tonight. May as well get some practice now."

But he knew he wouldn't be driving Elaine Dundry Todd home, when they saw the ambulance draw up to the mess ahead of them.

Blakeney-Smith waited on the steps, his Mae West slung over one shoulder and his flying helmet dangling from his hand.

"Where've you been?" Massey asked. "Don't you know there's a war on?"

"Hali the rear gunners in that little lot opened up on me together."

"That so?" Massey was totally uninterested.

"Every bloody one of them seemed to hit me, too."

"Too bad. We brought your car back."

"So I see. Thanks." Blakeney-Smith turned towards the door,

"How many d'you get?"

"One and two damaged." He threw the line away, over his shoulder. All in the day's work to the deadly Simon.

He was about to go indoors when Herrick, who had arrived after the others on his bicycle, called "Can I have a word with you, Simon?"

"De-briefing can wait till I've changed."

"Of course. Shall I come up to your room in half an hour?"

"My dear, I didn't know you cared! Come along now, if you like: you can drink my Scotch while I'm changing."

Sqdn Leader Maxwell drove home with his car windows open to the summer breeze.

He had taken command of 172 early in the year, after three months in France with another squadron at the beginning of the war. Once he and his wife had lived in large, comfortable married quarters, but now they were in a cottage near the aerodrome; and lucky to have found it. They still had the full-time services of a batman, and a daily woman from the village came for a couple of hours to do what he left undone; and to look after the child if they went out in the evenings. They kept open house for the squadron; for anyone on the station, in fact. A barrel of beer and several tankards and mugs were kept permanently on the front porch: Maxwell doctored it secretly with a bottle of rum. Everyone praised his beer and no one could understand why it was so much better than any in the pubs or the mess. It was the custom of the house for visitors to draw a pint before going in.

Betty was waiting for him on the lawn in front of the old cottage. Their eighteen-month-old-son tottered towards him and he picked him up. His wife got up from her deck chair and came to kiss him. He walked towards the house with one arm around her and the other holding his small boy.

"Busy day, darling." It was a comment, not a question, for she had heard and seen fighters taking off and returning since early morning.

"A good one, though. The boys did well."

She hugged him with the arm she had put about his waist. "Well done." Inwardly a great thankfulness and relief glowed in her: she knew that nobody had been killed or wounded that day; she always knew, from his look and his voice, however successfully he thought he was concealing his feelings. And she felt inadequate to all these occasions, whether good or bad: "well done" sounded as banal as congratulating a cricketer or a tennis player after a successful match; but what else could she say? He knew she was proud of the squadron, held them all in real affection, tried to get to know the new arrivals as quickly as she could and make them welcome in their home; was hurt when evil befell them and rejoiced when they went through a day's fighting unscathed. There was no need to voice any of that, and it would embarrass them both if she did. It was all right to say that she was proud of them, as she had done more than once: but it had to be said lightly, a throw-away. She couldn't say it at this moment, because she knew she would choke over the words. She had lived in tension throughout the day, had kept looking at the telephone, daring it to ring. And when it did, she had schooled herself not to rush to snatch it up.

He told her some of the trivial occurrences of the day: Sixgun's trick on Peter Knight with the bone, how Peter had retaliated later; family stories, at which she laughed with him.

The next half-hour was taken up by his son; helping to bath him and put him to bed, making sure that the private bulwark of normality with which they tacitly surrounded themselves remained secure.

They sat in the garden, afterwards, with their drinks. He took his wife's hand and smiled at her. "This is my kind of war."

She squeezed his hand, her heart full of too much emotion. Lightly, she said "Every home comfort."

"That's it. It hardly seems real. In France, we knew we were at war: it wasn't the living in tents, or requisitioned houses; it was the fact of being away from home. On foreign soil, as my grandfather used to say. And so utterly different from peacetime life. Even though we were among allies, it was all completely strange. But now we're home again and everything is so familiar, it's hard to believe we're actually as much on active service as we were in France. I don't feel any different from the City gents who take the train from East Malford every morning and come back with the London papers every evening."

She gave a small laugh. "It's not *quite* the same, darling." She was going to say that nobody was shooting at those City gents, but he would not like that.

"It's everybody's war. Those types who go up to Town every day curse when their trains are delayed by air raids: that's all the war means to them. They're just as likely to have a bomb dropped on them as we are."

She knew he was right. There wasn't room in the armed forces for everyone who volunteered: some who had done so were still waiting to join, sometimes delayed for several months. Others, feeling no dishonour, waited to be conscripted but would go willingly enough when their turn came. In the meanwhile there was nothing to do but carry on with their civilian jobs. The war had hardly changed their way of life.

Although the whole population of south-eastern England had experienced air raids, few related them to the airmen in uniform whom they saw around them. The residents of East Malford who went to London every day were used to the sight of air battles overhead and they read about them daily in the newspaper. But they did not know, when they saw a pilot in the village street or in a pub, that he was the man whom they had seen firing his guns fifteen thousand feet overhead, whose tracer bullets and vapour trails they had watched, from their office or train window, from shop or farmyard.

In the evenings, civilians and air crew rubbed shoulders in cinemas, restaurants, dance halls and pubs. Both were fundamentally doing the same thing: seeking relaxation at the end of a hard day's work. The civilians had lived through some danger too: railways, aerodromes, coastal radar sites, docks and engineering works were all targets for bombs, of which many fell on town, village and farm. The difference was that when they jostled a Hurricane or Spitfire pilot in the bar of the Mucky Duck or one of the other local pubs, they had merely washed off the grime of the City or the farm and were escaping from the boredom of files and figures or manual labour; whereas the pilots had come fresh from the smoke and terror of battle, with the stench of cordite still in their nostrils and their ears ringing with the din of gunfire and engines at full throttle. And that was *their* normal day's work.

Betty Maxwell said There's a strange kind of exhilaration in the air. Everybody knows we're all in it, and it seems to have drawn people closer together."

"That's why Hider can never beat us," her husband said quietly. "At the moment, this war is having to be fought almost entirely by the air force and the anti-aircraft boys. It's because we're so completely identified with the ordinary life that goes on around us that we've got a huge advantage over the enemy. The Germans are flying from strange bases in a hostile country: they've beaten France, but they must feel the hatred which surrounds them." He laughed apologetically for being solemn. "And, of course, there's the wonderful British disdain for foreigners: the ordinary man in the street doesn't think the Jerries have got a celluloid cat in hell's chance; just because they're only foreigners!"

"They seem to be reconciled to foreigners in Polish, French, and what-have-you, uniforms," Betty smiled. "The girls, anyway."

"That's just sympathy for the under-dog. They don't really believe they're as good as our own."

"Quite right," she said stoutly.

He laughed at her. "It's the commonplace life that's going on here which makes one feel so confident. As I was coming in to land just now, I saw people playing tennis at the local club: can you imagine them playing tennis on a summer evening if this were France or Germany? They'd be at panic stations. There'd be politicians bellowing at them through loudspeakers, exhorting them: *"courage mes amis"* and whatever that is in German; there'd be military bands everywhere and half the population would be lining the cliffs shaking their fists at the enemy. But here, we just take it all for granted. No dramatics."

Betty got up and put her arms around him and nuzzled her cheek against his. "I don't know about the ordinary man in the street, Max, but you sound pretty disdainful about foreigners yourself."

"Probably the greatest strength this country has is that, whereas in Germany the civilians believe their armed forces are invincible, here, our civilians *know* that *they're* never going to give in. They take it for granted our fighting Services are the best in the world. But they rely on themselves as much as on us."

We'll know soon enough, Betty thought: if the invasion comes; and when they start really bombing big cities.

But she knew, as her husband did, that the war was, so far, for most people, a huge adventure. A lot of men were happier in uniform than they had ever been. They had left humdrum jobs for a healthy, open-air life. Some, who had been clerks and trainees and salesmen, were better paid, and enjoyed higher social standing, as junior officers than ever before. Whether they were in the ranks or commissioned, they had comradeship, a new pride, freedom from the nagging worries of economic survival. Some welcomed new responsibility, others were as glad to rid themselves of it.

Betty Maxwell understood the strain under which her husband must be to have talked, even so deprecatingly, about his feelings: she was grateful to him for what he had told her; she knew the depth of his compassion and sensitivity, but during the past few weeks he had more and more hidden it under an almost callous-seeming manner; the customary British Service off-handedness, which she sometimes thought came near to puerile irreverence. There was nothing amusing or trivial about war, and it deserved to be accorded its own horrid dignity. She kissed him again, and said cheerfully "Are we going out?"

He responded quickly, his tired face breaking into a smile. "Indeed we are: the boys have got a very *rara avis* in tow tonight; you've got to meet her." He told her about the exotic and glamorous Elaine Dundry Todd.

In 1940, "compensation", "insecurity" and "virility symbol" had not yet become everyday jargon terms, but it was sometimes hinted that anyone who drove a sports car was likely to be doubtful of his potency and he who flaunted a big limousine was trying to reassure himself that he was as good as the next man. The truth, that some people just like sports cars and others enjoy the comfort of big, luxurious ones, was too dull to be worth printing.

Purveyors of half-baked psychology would have had a field day if they had taken their note books to the car park of the Spider's Web that evening.

Peter Knight's car was a third as old as himself: a Rover tourer with cut-away front doors which gave it an illusory sporting air. Being gregarious, he liked to have room for his friends, and the roomy old four-seater usually carried five or six.

Jumper Lee's would have confused anyone who maintained that an owner's character was reflected in his car: it was not rakish and dashing, but a sober and elderly Austin saloon; chosen for the roominess of its back seat.

The roadhouse was a phenomenon of the 'thirties, an attempt to bring sophistication to the rural fringes of the big towns; a neon-lit cross between pseudo-Tudor and concrete cubism, with the essential and superfluous swimming pool, where motorists could eat, drink and dance for faintly extortionate prices. Despite petrol rationing the Spider's Web was close enough to the big South London suburbs and several R.A.F. and Army camps in Kent and Surrey to continue in flourishing business. The blackout had doused the exterior illuminations, but it was lit up like a gin palace indoors.

Knight took Anne there when he felt opulent. He had brought her here on their first evening out, and she knew it was to impress her. She also knew that twenty-two-year-old flying officers could not afford to entertain often on that level. If they did so frequently, their motive was obvious. She had decided weeks before that Peter could have whatever he wanted, whenever he asked for it.

She would have preferred to dine alone with him, but she liked Six-gun and immediately approved of Elaine. She had never met an American woman before; but, from what she had heard of them on the talkies, had the impression that their normal speech was a brassy clangour. It was an agreeable surprise that Elaine's was low-pitched and smooth. Like everyone else, she had a soft spot for Jumper and admired his unquenchable *élan*, although she had reservations about his attitude to her sex. His girl of the week was a bit of a bore: a round-eyed (and presumably round-heeled) brunette who had just come back from a provincial tour of "White Horse Inn" and was talking vaguely about joining E.N.S.A.

Jumper's juices had begun to flow when he first saw Elaine Dundry Todd, and now that she had changed into a fresh dark blue, gold braided, A.T.A. uniform and scented herself with a perfume that was quite different from the aroma of flying machines which had lingered with her out at dispersals, she made him fidgety. His dark-eyed actress or dancing girl accepted the straying of his attention with aplomb: there was no lack of men, and she rather fancied both Peter and Six-gun.

"How did you come to join the A.T.A.?" asked Jumper. "Did you come over from America specially to join?"

"Not really. I'd done some air racing and rallying and here I was living in England, with a British husband… "

"Does he fly?"

She looked amused. "A bit, yes."

"You mean he's an enthusiastic amateur?"

"He's certainly enthusiastic, but I guess he's not strictly an amateur."

"Airline pilot?" asked Massey.

She shook her head and looked mischievous.

Knight saw that his friends realised they had put their feet in it somewhere, and was enjoying their growing discomfort. In happy anticipation, he said "Tell us the worst."

"Well… as a matter of fact, he's Chief Flying Instructor at an operational training unit."

"Oh, my God!" Massey rolled his eyes up to heaven. "I'm seducing a squadron leader's wife."

"Wing Commander's, honey," she corrected him sweetly. Six-gun pretended to hide under the table, while the rest of them laughed at his discomfiture.

Mrs Wing Commander Todd went on: "They turned us out of our nice married quarters, and we could only find some horrid damp old thatched cottage to rent, and George – my husband – is so busy I just never get to see him, so I thought I might as well make myself useful in the A.T.A. Of course," she added, looking directly at Massey, "if he were on an operational station I'd have stayed right there with him, because I think that's a wife's place if her husband's on ops. But George is too *old* for operational flying now, so I guess I'll be staying with the A.T.A. And when he gets posted overseas I'll be glad to have this to keep me occupied." Her emphasis on "old" was meaningful.

She put her hand on Massey's thigh, under the table, and he quickly moved his own to hold it. The pact was sealed. He was going to be all right this evening, after all, despite that queasy moment of doubt. Hail Columbia! This broad… pardon, this gal, knew where her war work really lay: bless her patriotic little heart.

After dinner the rest of the squadron turned up. The extra sleep the night before had renewed their energy and the whole day had seemed, in an odd way, a refreshment. The arrival of brand new replacement aircraft, the zeal of a fresh squadron in the wing, the day's successes: each had brought encouragement and added confidence. On some evenings everyone was in bed an hour after dinner; on others, there was a noisy surge all the way to London and a round of nightclubs. Some pilots lived quietly all the time, others flogged their wilting minds and bodies through hour after hour of drinking, dancing and womanising, night after night. 172 was a squadron which hung very much together and Maxwell set the mood. Tonight they were all out on the town, Maxwell, Poynter and Bernie Harmon with their wives, the others alone or with girl friends.

Nigel Cunningham and Roddy Webb sipped their beer, blushed whenever one of the girls spoke to them, charmed Betty Maxwell and Blaine, and drew long, suspicious looks from Jumper Lee's musical comedy actress. She breathed a gin-slurred question in his ear when they were dancing: "Who are the two fairies?"

"No fairies on this squadron." Jumper bristled

"No? You just go and ask one of those two young queens if he'll give you a dance; you'd be surprised." She buried her face in his shoulder to hide her giggles.

Flight Lieutenant Lee took a poor view. This bit of crackling was treading on very dicey ground. He didn't want to be acid, but there were some things one didn't say; outsiders certainly didn't say them about the squadron.

"They're shy. And they've got good manners: I don't suppose you come across either very much in your job."

"Ouch! I asked for that. *I'll* ask them to dance; that should break down their shyness."

"If *you* can't, nothing will."

"Darling, you're being rather horrid tonight."

The Squadron M.O. looked on with professional interest and concern. God alone knew where Lee generated his inexhaustible energy; he was a phenomenon, he defied medical science and should have been either a palsied wreck, taking so much out of himself, or as unresponsive as a block of marble to be able to do so. He was neither. His reactions were fast, he flew brilliantly, ate heartily and slept well. The doctor sighed. Born military leaders not infrequently manifested a vast sexual, capacity: Napoleon, Wellington and Nelson had never gone short of mistresses; he could envy them; comprehending them was something else.

He watched Harmon for a few moments, dancing with his wife and laughing palely with her like a schoolboy staying up too late at his first dinner-jacket party. Not a very good simile, perhaps, for an East End urchin who had certainly never possessed a dinner jacket and would very probably not live to do so. And if he looked like a child, that was where the common factor ended. Harmon was as complex a puzzle as Jumper Lee: but at least a doctor could put his finger on the reason why he was what he was. Young Bernie's instinct for self-preservation was so strongly developed that it was primitive and entirely unconscious. Other people attributed his success and survival to his fantastic sense of timing, but the doctor knew that this was not a cause but an effect Harmon's frail look and natural pallor were misleading, too. He ate like a horse and the muscles stood out on this thin body hard and well defined; the Apprentices' School had taken care of that. The M.O. wondered when Harmon had last felt afraid.

He knew that Blakeney-Smith lived in constant fear, and that was why he was so aggressive and flamboyant, so competitive and tried so hard to be the complete extrovert. His ruinous fundamental insecurity, as much as his genes, had made him a coward; an irredeemable one. But he had to fly and he had to fight when his aircraft was serviceable and he was under orders, he could not back out. When he was in the air he could not run away. The doctor, with all his intelligence, did not know how much alone a man could be in a crowded sky and a running fight, how easy it was in reality to turn tail. But, at least for the time being, Blakeney-Smith was doing all right with his A.T.S. officer, a necessary distraction, and the M.O. sucked contentedly on his pipe.

Dunal was well away, too. That was not to be wondered at: British girls had romantic ideas about Frenchmen; the very word "French" had limitless libidinous implications. Pierre was a Frenchman, therefore he must be a formidable lover; they fell over themselves to get at him first He chain-smoked, looked at them invitingly from under his heavy-lidded eyes, twitched the comer of his mouth seductively from time to time, no doubt thought what boring little bitches they were, and took everything they offered. The doctor asked himself whether Dunal possessed them with the violence with which he set out to kill Germans. It was a personal fight for him, in a way which the British did not share, and it would be the cause, one day soon, of his death.

Lotnikski flew with hatred and despair, too, and he went after women with the same dreadful zest. He was an animal when he had taken too much drink, like a randy stallion which only wanted to mount the nearest mare and would tear her to pieces if she resisted. He was the despair of the gentle, experienced senior W.A.A.F. officer, the "Queen Bee", who knew what happened to any of her girls who was alone with him after dark. The doctor knew what happened, too, and how easy it was for the handsome, relentless foreigner, with his fascinating accent, to excite the sympathy and romanticism of young working-class girls who had never been more than a hundred miles from home. He was both pathetic and glamorous: far from home, bereft of family and exotically sophisticated. Here was another man who smelt of death and made the M.O. bite hard on his pipe stem.

The best of them could crack and sometimes it was the best of them who did: the ones like Lee, Knight, Poynter or Massey; because they were so physically sound and emotionally stable that they would go on stretching themselves further and further, until the breakdown came without warning.

It was not only the fighting, but the waiting, the frustration of bad weather, false alarms, errors of controlling, all the irritants which were even more frequent than actual combat, although that was a daily experience too, which were abrasive to the nerves of fighting men.

The doctor exchanged glances with Herrick, who held his eye and nodded. Journalists were not admitted to the freemasonry of the medical profession, but the Intelligence Officer and he had a special understanding. Spy was a good journalist, not a sensation-monger; he had a true feeling for the squadron's stresses and respected their reticences. Wild horses would not have dragged the doctor into the cockpit of a combat aircraft, but Herrick was perpetually and mournfully half-aware of his life's greatest regret: he was thwarted, by inadequate vision and a history of chest ailments, from flying. He and the M.O. shared confidences, with each other and with the young pilots.

When Herrick prayed he asked God to warm the hearts of the Air Council towards those with astigmatic eyes and a less than perfectly efficient pair of lungs.

The M.O., a sardonic man, did not pray at all. Nor did many of the pilots. Blakeney-Smith did, and then it was only through fear.

The Spider's Web was closed. A large old Austin saloon stood in a field entrance, under some trees. Its springs began to wheeze and squeak as the coachwork rocked gently in rhythm with the close-coupled movement of Flight Lieutenant Lee and his sloe-eyed chorus girl.

On camp, Six-gun Massey crept upstairs with his shoes in one hand, the fingers of his other entwined with those of Mrs Elaine Dun dry Todd, as she led him through the darkness of a strange house. Everyone else was asleep and neither of them knew when a creaking stair might betray them. With as much caution as though he were stalking a Heinkel through broken cloud, Massey glided along the upstairs corridor, following another man's wife to her bedroom. He was a brave man, but would only dare to do this behind her husband's back. Her husband, however, was not much in either of their thoughts.

She opened her door and shut it behind them and the only sound they made was their heavy breathing. There was a pause in the blacked out room before they found each other. Not a long pause.

Tuttle and the country girl from No. 1 O.M.Q. strolled towards the camp gates with their arms about each other. She had to check in at the W.A.A.F. Guard Room before going to her quarters and Tuttle waited for her. 'Alf a pint o' cyder on top of a double gin and orange ought to 've done the trick. She was only a kid, not used to drinking. Ought to be all right for a bit o' grumble-an'-grunt tonight, then.

He saw her come towards him and went to meet her. "You bein' new 'ere, an' all, I oughter shew yer where the nearest air raid shelter is. Yer never know when the siren's goin' ter go, one night…"

He put his arm around her waist but she pulled away. "You are awful. Me mother warned me about boys like you. Thank you ever so for taking me out, Norm; I did have ever such a nice time." She kissed him, clumsily but with enthusiasm, on his mouth, which was half-open with surprise, and he heard the patter of her running feet.

"Well Oi'll be booggered!" Still, there was always tomorrow night.

Dunal was not refused, however. He had picked up a girl at the Spider's Web, a secretary in some local office, and gone with her to her bed-sitter. He was bored and tired, and habitually contemptuous. He did not stay long in her bed and when he left her he had done more for her patriotism than any number of enemy air raids: My Gawd, if that damp little squib's what they call a marvellous French lover, give me an English boy any time.

Lotnikski was with a woman, too, another road house pickup; but this one was higher in the economic scale than Dunal's and had a car. Her husband was with his regiment in the Outer Hebrides and she took her new Polish friend home to their detached Jerry-built house in a quiet road. The blackout gave them immunity from the embarrassment of street lights and inquisitive neighbours. Within three minutes of going upstairs she began to yelp and when he set out to walk back to the Spider's Web, where he had left his bicycle, she felt as though she had been through a typhoon in an open boat; she might have borne some of the same scars if she had: her lip was bleeding and there was a bite on her shoulder, her ribs were bruised and her pelvis felt crushed. But she was already looking forward to the next night with him and lay with a smile both reminiscent and anticipatory until she fell asleep.

Knight had dropped Massey and his lady aviator at the end of the Officers' Mess road. Now Anne moved closer to him and laid her head on his shoulder. When they came to her home he stopped the car on the grass verge outside the gate. "Don't want to disturb your people."

"You will come in, won't you?"

He kissed her first. "What do *you* think?"

They walked hand-in-hand up the drive and when they entered the darkened house there was a torch on the hall table to light them. She checked that the curtains in the drawing room were drawn close, then switched on a heavily shaded table lamp. Knight felt at home. The room, with its conventional chintz-covered sofa and armchairs, its well polished antique mahogany tables and display cabinets, its silver vases and photograph frames, was a replica of his own parents' drawing room. It smelt the same, with the faint lavender odour of furniture cream and the scent of the same flowers as they would have at this time of year. The bow window at one end and the french window at the other were as familiar to him as though he had always lived here.

The girl stood near and he drew her close against him to kiss hex again. They sat with their arms around each other on the sofa.

"Thank you for a lovely evening, Peter."

"I'm glad you liked Elaine. I wasn't sure about her at first."

"She's fun. And very brave and clever to fly so many different kinds... types of aircraft all over the place. I really ought to do something instead of staying at home."

"You're not serious?" He was troubled.

"It's on my conscience, Peter."

"But your voluntary work at the hospital..."

"That's not much. And it's not directly helping the war effort..."

"I don't think the wounded types in the hospital would be very flattered!"

"It's selfish of me. I just don't want to leave home as long as you're here."

He said nothing for a while, holding her firmly to him and resting his cheek against her hair, soft and fragrant and infinitely stirring, so that he was overwhelmed at die same time by protectiveness and a desire to strip her naked.

"You know I want to marry you, Anne."

She turned in his arms, moved her head back and smiled into his face. "You've never said so."

"It wouldn't be fair. I might..." he hesitated. "I might get an overseas posting, and the war's going to go on a long time." Poor darling: I might... might get an overseas posting. I might be killed was what he meant. And he didn't say so, to spare her rather than himself.

"I'll marry you tomorrow if you want me to, darling."

"I want you to, darling; but we can't."

Thus do the British do their courting and make their declaration of undying love and passion!

A few miles away, Simon Blakeney-Smith was offering no resistance to his officer lady's importunities. They were both comfortably tight and staggered a little and giggled as they undressed one another in the cramped little room she occupied in a wooden hut on a dreary new A.T.S. barracks site.

"Rotten example to the girls, aren't I?"

"Damned good example. Should be a lot more of this, to help the war effort." He fell heavily on her bed. "Come here, you."

Her breath was sour and tainted with nicotine. He remembered the fresh young F.A.N.Y. in the ambulance. But this would have to do for now.

They had enjoyed themselves in Boulogne. The blonde, the redhead and a couple of nondescripts had gone with Hafner, Ihlefeld and two other pilots, Weber and Baumbach. Dinner was quiet and well behaved, eaten with Teutonic concentration on the pleasures of the stomach which discouraged the girls from chatter. But by the end of it all eight of them were flushed and growing noisy. They sat at a comer table, among other Germans, isolated from the rest of the room. There were many German officers in the restaurant, some of them with French women; but apart from the obligatory heel-click-ing and bowing to their superiors, none acknowledged the others. The French pointedly looked the other way.

They blundered noisily into the farmhouse, the girls already half-undressed and laughing shrilly. There was some dispute about who would go with whom and finally Hafner took the redhead and left the blonde with, Ihlefeld while the others argued drunkenly.

Greiner, sitting in the big kitchen with the widow Proud-homme, contentedly smoking his pipe, drinking coffee and, with her help, reading a French newspaper, heard than come in and jumped to his feet.

She looked at him scornfully. "Where are you going, Monsieur Greiner?"

"Nowhere, Madame. I'm only listening: he may need help. I often have to undress him."

"I know." Her tone was heavy with contempt. "But you can hear that he won't need you to do that for him tonight; there are other willing hands."

"French hands," he reminded her; not without hope.

She spat into the rubbish pail by the stove but did not reply.

They heard dragging footsteps overhead and the slamming of doors, the creak of bedsprings.

Greiner sat down again and picked up his paper. Covertly he glanced at the woman. With compressed lips she glared at her knitting. In resignation he put aside the newspaper and trudged off to his lonely bed in the barn.

BERNIE HARMON HAD CEASED TO BE AFRAID.

Just as love can teach a man to hate, joy can make him miserable and despair turn him into a martyr, so a succession of experiences of total terror can, if survived, give him conscious immunity from fear.

Harmon woke early the next morning and his first thought was that he welcomed the day. He looked forward to the fighting it would bring.

This was not a sublimation of fear, not an instance of the truism that the bravest man is the one who is afraid but conquers his fear; that only a stupid, insensitive man can be unafraid, thus his acts of apparent bravery do not qualify, because he is not overcoming a weakness. Harmon's was a sublime self-confidence, acquired by passing through many mortal dangers in triumph. He knew his own quality as pilot and marksman and knew that nature had given him eyesight and timing of extraordinary sharpness. He was equipped with the best fighter aircraft in the world, if properly handled. He could see no reason to be afraid any longer.

When he had first met the enemy he felt sick with fright. He had gone on feeling frightened until he had fought in twelve engagements and shot down three bombers and three Me. 109s. At that point his fear suddenly vanished. Now it cost him nothing, emotionally, to go into action. He had come to enjoy destruction. Other fighter pilots with whom he had tried to talk about attitudes to destroying an enemy aircraft had all backed away and dismissed the matter in the same embarrassed terms: they never thought of it as a fight against another human being; as killing someone. It was simply one machine against another.

But to him, since he had first shot down a German aeroplane at the age of nineteen, it had always been personal combat of the medieval and most basic sort: man against man; never a mere impersonal contest between a Hurricane and a Messerschmitt or Heinkel. He had not yet admitted to himself that he was intent on killing: he believed still that all he wanted was to shoot enemy airmen down to put them out of action.

When he spoke on the R/T, once he had sighted the enemy, his voice rose and became fixed on a note which suggested hypnosis. With each succeeding call he made, during an interception, its pitch went up until it reached a shrillness that could sound almost demented. The only ones who had registered the change which came over him were the Operations Room controllers who talked to him on the radio, guided him towards the enemy, listened to his comments when a fight was over, and helped him back to base.

Once, the Senior Controller at East Malford had controlled him on a long pursuit through broken cloud in the fading light of a wet evening in early summer, when communication between controller and pilot became more a communion, in the intimacy and singleness of purpose which it demanded and provoked. A solitary enemy raider had sneaked over the coast and a single fighter was scrambled to intercept it. Harmon's increasing excitement, tension and concentration had communicated themselves to the controller, who felt himself tingling and sweating from vicarious participation in what he recognised was a murderous lust to kill the men in the Dornier, not merely a determination to bring down the bomber itself. He was told afterwards that his face became a mask, as though he were in a trance. He had made some self-conscious and jocular comment about being mesmerised by the sense of responsibility, but he brooded on it for a long time and decided that "trance" was a good word to describe what happened to young Flight Sergeant Harmon. Now, many combats and many kills later, Pilot Officer Harmon still lost himself in a kind of self-hypnosis when killing time was near.

Bernie did not know any of this about himself. He only knew that it was a deep relief to be afraid no longer. He recognised his satisfaction in destroying the enemy fighter pilots and air gunners who were trying to kill him, and the bomber pilots who were trying to devastate his country, but rationalised this as the natural human instinct for self-preservation. He did not hate them for being Germans or because they were Nazis. He shot them down with conscious relish because he knew what they were trying to do to him and to his country: it was not machines that were trying to kill him and reduce England to ruins, but the men who flew them.

The cause of his lethal frenzy did not matter as much as its effect: he was now immune from the fear which was felt by his comrades, who were ordinary young men without the touch of genius or talent or whatever the quality is which sets men apart from their fellows, and which made Harmon a supremely efficient and ruthless killing machine.

There were other things that he enjoyed: rifle and clay pigeon shooting, at which he was brilliant; table tennis, where his lightning reactions and deadly accuracy had made him a champion. At shooting and table tennis a man did not have to be big, strong or fit, to excel. It was skill and timing which gave him superiority; just as in air fighting.

Most of all he enjoyed making love to his wife. He turned and contemplated her now: small, pigeon-plump, with a rosebud mouth and long lashes resting on rosy cheeks. He buried his thin, small hand – dancing with Bernie was like holding a bird's claw, Anne Holt said – in her long, dark hair and kissed her into wakefulness. Smiling sleepily in anticipation, Sarah took him in her arms and shifted cosily around.

Later they both ate a breakfast such as few people in Britain then, with food rationing, could indulge themselves in. They lived in two rooms over a butcher's shop, which they had chosen not so much for proximity to the airfield and a low rent as for the ease and secrecy with which meat beyond the legal ration could be taken upstairs. And the butcher, naturally, was related to the grocer.

As usual, Bernie Harmon cycled into dispersals a good quarter of an hour before the other pilots appeared.

He went straight to his aircraft and was soon the centre of a group of ground crew, chatting and joking with them on terms of easy equality. He had been a technician himself, when he passed out of apprentice school, and until very recently an N.C.O.: there were no barriers between him and any of them, just as there were no barriers between him and his brother officers.

One of the new Hurricanes was standing next to his.

He noticed that Blakeney-Smith's personal insignia had already been stencilled on to it: a mailed fist holding a battle-axe. "The family crest, actually, old boy," as Simon had explained; and been met by Peter Knight's acid "Which family old boy: the Blakeneys or the Smiths? Surely the Smiths' should be a bloody anvil? And isn't a blakeney something you mend shoes with?"

Even the absurd Simon had not been so crass as to prolong the matter by pointing out that those were blakeys.

Bernie Harmon, the only natural, and most accomplished, killer at East Malford, did not bother with defiant decorations on his aircraft. He sometimes thought that he might let the ground crew paint a Mickey Mouse on it; perhaps even Mickey cocking a snook or sticking up two fingers. But nothing in the nature of a line-shoot like heraldry or belligerent caricatures. At the back of his mind was a vague intention to indulge himself in some whimsy when his score of confirmed kills reached twenty. If he had thought about that a bit he might have perceived a hint of superstition in it, but the idea never occurred to him. Meanwhile he humoured the erks by allowing them to mark his score on the fuselage in the customary way; he was uninterested in this display, but it kept them happy.

Hafner stood morosely under the shower, with an aching head.

Presently Weber shuffled in, yawning. "My God! These French frippets make me appreciate my wife more than ever. I wish to God I could go home on leave."

Baumbach, on his heels, agreed. "Makes me appreciate my fiancee, too, when these empty-headed French bitches make themselves so cheap. I can't stand drunken women. And some of the things they want to do in bed! Damned disgusting…"

"I'll take the burden off you," one of the others offered with a laugh.

Another said "Yeah, and we ought to find some other way to make Weber appreciate his wife, too. I'll take that piece off your hands, Johann, if you like…"

"Go and take a running screw at yourself."

"I may have to! I haven't found a girl who appealed to me for at least two weeks."

Ihlefeld lurched in. "God, I feel grim this morning. That blonde's insatiable, Erich."

"You'd better have the redhead back, then: I managed to satisfy the blonde easily enough!"

The two-week celibate asked, "You or that randy Alsatian of yours?"

It was the kind of remark which appealed to the German sense of humour and set everyone guffawing and elaborating on the theme. Only a joke about excreta could have amused them more. So much for Teutonic fun.

They went to breakfast with their usual ravenous young appetites, despite the punishment they had inflicted on their stomachs the previous evening. All they remembered were the pleasures of the night; its miseries were already forgotten.

Greiner watched them strut towards the mess and shook his head tolerantly. What a bunch of lads they were! Living for the moment, careless of what the immediate future held in store. Even the best was not good enough for these fine young gentlemen. What stories he would have to tell around the fireside when this was all over: Yes, I knew General Hafner when he was a young lieutenant. He remembers me well: every year, at the old comrades' reunion, he has a word with me. That's right, the same General Hafner who commands the British Air Force: good allies, those British, now that they have settled down under the Führer as a German colony.

But they hadn't won the war yet. And Leutnant Hafner may not be one of those destined to survive it, despite his papally-blessed medal. Poor young devil, how could anyone begrudge him his pleasures?

He set about tidying the disorder in the room.

They were all far from home, Greiner told himself, strangers in a hostile land, and it must be much worse for the youngsters than it was for the likes of him. He could find a certain philosophy of outlook, at his age; and he was not accustomed to much, at the best of times: unlike the officer-gentry.

A more than philosophical gleam lit his eyes as he thought ahead to the moment when he could take a respite from his work and go out to the fields to give Madame Prudhomme a hand on the farm.

Richter saw the group of younger men enter the dining-room and wondered how they could look so spry after their orgy. He had heard their noisy return and the sound of girls' voices.

He glowered round the table and said, tight-lipped: "Your formation flying is going to pieces. It is the responsibility of Schwarm leaders to ensure that their sections hold correct position. If there is not a great improvement today I shall send some of you back to flying school for further training."

There was a resentful silence. What had suddenly made the Old Man so liverish? If it was a woman he needed, why hadn't he said so last night? It would have been easy enough to fix him up.

The first scramble came at eight-thirty. 172 were at readiness, some of them muzzy again with sleep after waking from a late night and breakfasting: they had settled down to doze in the thin sunlight when the telephone brought them to their feet with hearts thudding. They took off in full squadron strength, twelve Hurricanes bellowing, charging like bulls dashing into the arena, across the aerodrome and out of sight over the hangar roofs.

This was no false alarm: neither a feint by the enemy nor some vagary of the radar. The sky was thick with enemy aircraft. Maxwell led his squadron in well rehearsed attacks by sections, each wing man covering his leader instead of breaking for individual attacks. They shot down four bombers in their first pass, then the fighters were among them and they had to break and it was every man for himself.

They came back singly and in occasional pairs; eleven of them. One of the pilots who had been absent the day before, on compassionate leave, was back with the squadron this morning. Knight and others saw him half-roll and dive after an attack on a

Heinkel and fly headlong into an Me. 109 as it pulled up and away from a Spitfire it had set on lire. This was the first time that one of their own squadron had been lost in a collision and it upset them all by its sheer ill luck.

Not even bad flying could be blamed for it: it was an accident and a senseless way to die. Gunfire was an occupational hazard to which they were long inured, but this was downright bad luck and damned unfair. It made them bad tempered and sour and when they landed they were quiet, morose, their hands unsteady. Dunal smoked furiously, his fingers trembling. Blakeney-Smith walked away to hide the wavering flame of his lighter, which he had to hold with both hands to his cheroot. Flight Sergeant Viccar spilled a mug of tea and Knight dropped the apple which Massey lobbed at him in an easy catch.

They were spread about the grass in low-murmuring or silent clusters when a strange Hurricane landed and surprised them by taxiing over to their dispersal.

When the pilot stepped out of it, Cunningham and Webb, recognising him, leaped up from their deck chairs. But he walked directly to the C.O. and two flight commanders, who were talking to Herrick, and came to attention awkwardly in his flying boots. "Good morning, sir. My name's Gifford." He was diffident and fresh-faced, a tall, broad-shouldered boy who should have been in school, not butchering his fellow men or being butchered. Like thousands of others of his generation; and his father's before him.

Maxwell and the two flight lieutenants looked him up and down casually. The C.O. said "Glad to have you. Welcome to the squadron. Glad to see you brought your own aircraft with you: that'll make the plumber happy." He introduced Poynter and Lee. "We got word of your posting rather late last evening, but you'll find a room ready for you in the mess."

"Thank you, sir. I'll go over later. I'd rather stick around here if… if it's all right, sir. I was made operational yesterday." He went brick red, as though guilty of a breach of convention.

Over-eagerness was not the most admired trait in a newcomer's character.

The two flight commanders exchanged glances: here was a trained man they could both use.

Maxwell spoke kindly. "Settle down and we'll see what we can do for you. Introduce him to the boys, Jumper."

"I know those two," Gifford pointed. "Did all my training with them." Webb and Cunningham were eyeing him like a couple of gun dogs, their noses almost twitching.

When he had made a quick round of the rest of the pilots with Lee, he joined his friends. "What are you doing here, Patrick?" Webb asked.

"The squadron I was posted to is converting from Hurricanes to cannon-armed Spitfires: they moved to Scotland today to do their familiarisation. As I'd barely had four hours' flying on the squadron, on Hurricanes, they posted me here, where they thought I'd be more use."

"We're still waiting to go operational," Cunningham said glumly. "I suppose you've been on ops already?"

"No, but I am operational"

"Lucky devil. D'you hear that, Roddy?"

"Luck of the draw. We're busy here: no time to spare for sprogs like us. You were lucky to go to a squadron in a quiet sector, Patrick. Anyway, what the hell's the use of being operational if you didn't actually get the chance to go on ops?"

"Yes, by God: once we are made operational here we won't have to hang around."

But they hung around for the rest of the morning; all three of them. The second scramble sent "B" Flight's six aircraft southward while "A" Flight kicked their heels. Forty minutes later, four came back.

Then another squadron scramble, and one pilot missing.

The newly arrived Gifford was detailed for the next sortie, as weaver at the rear of the formation, with orders to keep his eyes peeled for surprise attacks out of the sun.

"Lucky sod," envied Webb. And the lucky sod pinkened with pleasure at the compliment of being taken on trust because he came from a good squadron under a sound commander known to Maxwell. He sat leaning forward in his chair, ready to sprint, glancing every now and then towards the hut from which the telepone message would come.

When it did, he almost beat Blakeney-Smith in the dash to their cockpits.

After the Hurricanes had gone it was quiet and deserted at dispersals, with only a wireless set in the workshop breaking the silence, and the clatter of a farmer's tractor in the distance. The station cricket pitch was across the road and the homely smell of newly mown grass was carried on the warm breeze.

"Bet he gets a Jerry first time out, too," Cunningham said.

But it was the other way round, and when the eleven who came back had landed, the story was told.

Maxwell was the last down and his first question was: "Anyone see what happened to Gifford?"

Cunningham felt the sweat break out on his body and his heart seem to swell until it would burst out of his chest. Webb had the urge to go quickly to the latrine, but pressed his legs together and waited.

"I saw him get well and truly bounced, sir." Flight Sergeant Viccar, his face drawn and streaked with oil and smoke from a shell explosion in his cockpit, dragged on a cigarette. "He'd been weaving bloody well and hanging on." He turned to Sergeant Wilkins. "Right, Wilkie?"

"Too true. He had his finger right out We made two attacks and then he seemed to get confused in the break. I looked round and he'd got left behind. Then two 109s bounced him and he just blew up."

Maxwell nodded dourly and glanced about. He caught the eyes of Gifford's two friends and turned abruptly away.

"He hadn't even been to the mess to book in," Webb muttered. "It's just as though he was never here at all."

Subdued and frightened, they went back to their patch of grass in the sun. But Knight was coming for them: "Come on, you two. I'm not on the next detail. I'm taking you up and if you're O.K. you'll be operational."

With less swiftness than they would have shewn an hour earlier, they went with him,

Tuttle went about his work whistling. He had got over his disappointment of the night before and decided to look on the bright side and regard the money he had spent on buying the girl a couple of drinks as an investment. It would accumulate. He'd try again tonight and if he had no luck he would try again tomorrow. Eventually he'd get it in.

He looked in the pockets of Knight's best blue but there was nothing interesting or incriminating in them.

Tuttle opened the top drawer of the dressing table and found a letter from Knight's father which he instantly opened.

"Dear Peter, I know you always find life a trifle pressing towards the end of the month, and as I happened to have quite a decent win at my bookmaker's expense yesterday, I'm enclosing a fiver which you may find useful for taking some nice girl out to dinner. Mother and I are looking forward so much to your next leave. It does seem a long time since you were home. Even a week-end would be something. You must be feeling the strain of things..."

And so it went on; family news and messages of affection. Tuttle was too insensitive to perceive the love, pride and anxiety behind Dr Knight's words.

He was disappointed. Some of the officers had much more interesting correspondents. Like most batmen, he was a shameless reader of private mail, bank statements and bills. He knew which officers always carried contraceptives and when they used them. He knew the financial situation of nearly every officer on the station: although he only looked after four of them he gossiped with the other servants. Some incautious Operations Room controller had left a pregnant Land Army girl behind when he was posted from his last station, and she wrote in panic to him almost every day; the batmen were making bets on whether she would complain to the Station Commander, or even find a way to tell the controller's wife. As the latter wrote to him affectionately almost every day as well, the mess servants following this drama with particular interest.

Tuttle had no qualms about prying into other people's private affairs. He regarded the opportunity to do so as one of the perquisites of his lowly job. After all, if he had to clean their shoes and make out their laundry lists and do all sorts of demeaning jobs, they must expect to provide him with a little amusement in return. Besides, no booger sent *him* five quid because it was a long time to pay day.

THE DAY WAS NO SHORTER OR LESS HARD FOR II JG
97 than for their enemies on the other side of the English Channel.
But their mood was not the same.

On their first mission, well rested and invigorated by a stinging
shower and a good breakfast, most of them sang as they climbed to
form a screen around the bombers which forged towards England.

It gave them great pride to be part of this display of German
might. It could not be long now before the British gave in. They
knew that after this raid there would be another, and another after
that, then a fourth and a fifth; and a tenth, if need be. The attacks
would go on all night if they must, for the factories of the Reich could
undoubtedly replace threefold every bomber or fighter shot down.

To be part of this huge array of destructive force gave the
German airmen a sense of inviolability and invincibility. They
were as effectively hypnotised as African savages who are told by
witch doctors that the charms they carry make them impervious to
the weapons of an enemy.

But Richter's pilots remembered his earlier strictures and the
Schwarm leaders barked at their formations to fly with care and
precision. He must not have cause to criticise them again.

This time, surely, they would destroy their targets. Today the
airfields they attacked would be put out of action: their buildings
razed and the occupants killed, the Hurricanes and Spitfires caught
in hangars and on the dispersal lines set on fire, riddled with bullets,
blown up; or shot down as they tried vainly to fly out of danger. No

matter how heavy an air raid, the crazy R.A.F. ran to their fighters and tried to get them into the air and away from the falling bombs.

Hafner hummed contentedly. Let the Tommies come! They were good fighters but there were not enough of them. In every encounter they were outnumbered at least three to one.

The long, slow bum of perpetual but sometimes subconscious resentment reached the explosive charge of his personal hatred: with luck, he would see the Hurricane for which he always kept his eyes peeled now. YZ-E, with the insulting, swastika-chewing mongrel on its nose, was his pet hate. He felt no chivalry towards its pilot; to shoot him down, he would join a dozen other Me. 109s, even if the Hurricane were already falling in flames, for the satisfaction of putting in one burst himself.

He wondered what sort of man it was who flew it: some puny fellow with thin white limbs and a stupid pride in his deliberate amateurism; a typically frivolous Englishman who treated war as a sport and was delighted when he nicked an Me. 109 with a few lucky shots; and even more gratified to return home with a whole skin. But making war was not a sport, however the foolish British may try to turn it into one; it was a profession and only professional warriors could survive.

The bombers were splitting up and No. 1 Staffel swung westward at a curt command from Richter.

In a moment the air was full of warning cries.

"Achtung! Red Indians high right…"

"Break left, break left!"

"Behind you, Franz…"

"I'm hit… I'm hit…"

"Holy God! I'm on fire… My hood's jammed…"

Screams of terror and agony from men dying, wounded, burning, trapped.

Suddenly the air fleet of many hundreds did not seem so irresistible or the crews so bullet-proof.

Hafner twisted his body in its tight straps, trying to scan the whole sky, nerves jangling. Why didn't Richter order a break?

Then the shouted command and howling engines, the flash of sunlight on the pale undersides of wings and fuselages as the Staffel whipped over and down in a last-second attempt to get behind the Hurricanes which had taken them unawares out of the sun.

And that was only the start of that day's work. They landed, refuelled and re-armed; and with only twenty minutes respite were airborne again. They returned a second time to base, badly mauled by the R.A.F. They waited in sullen little groups for the return of comrades who would never come back. The morning cost them five aircraft, two lives, two prisoners and one severely wounded.

What had gone wrong with the incantations of their witch doctors?

Connie Gates was on her rounds. It was lunch time and the back of the van was loaded with the best that the Officers' Mess could provide. She knew what good food did for people and was glad that she could help in this way. She would have been better pleased if she could have tipped a bottle of rum into each urn of coffee. She was sure that Drake hadn't fought the Armada on so weak a brew.

There were new faces almost every day, and different tensions: sometimes everyone was jumpy, although they tried not to shew it, because casualties were bad; sometimes they were as nappy as highly-strung racehorses, and made no attempt to conceal it, because they were eager to get back into the air without wasting time on the ground: that was when things were going well for them. She knew it only meant that some other wing was losing pilots that day and their own turn would come again too soon; but it was enough to change the whole atmosphere of each dispersal area.

This morning there was a sense of strain, but no sombre, weary silence. If they were quiet it was a satisfied, resting quietness; a gathering of strength for the next battle, not a licking of wounds from the last.

She saw the two shy ones who were beginning to concern her. They looked like boys who had been robbing an orchard: grime on their hands and faces, clothes rumpled, tired in the way that anyone is tired after a long period of enforced alertness; but as though the apples had been worth stealing, even though the angry farmer with his heavy stick had caught them a clout or two. She felt pity for them because she knew, in some ways better than they did, what they were up against. Her reasoning was completely un-complicated and feminine, if logical: what chance had these boys, with so little experience, got against grown German men who had been preparing to fight this war for years?

But they were officers and she was a mess servant and her job was to feed them, not be their mother or mistress; willingly though she played the latter part whenever she was able and the fortunate lover deserving enough.

She showed off her legs and her bosom in her usual brisk, cheerful way and drew the familiar glances and precious secret smiles of the favoured few who knew the softness and warmth and mystery hidden beneath her freshly ironed appearance and respectful, efficient manner.

The ground defence machine-gun crews in their sandbagged emplacements watched her with envy. They were only paid three or four shillings a day, whereas sergeant pilots got twelve-and-six, and when the enemy attacked the airfield they would be more vulnerable than the pilots, who could at least run for their fighters and try to take them up, or dive for shelter underground. But the freshly made and thickly filled sandwiches and good coffee were not for the humble ground gunners. They would have to wait their turn in the cookhouse and be grateful for whatever meagre ration of meat and abundance of potatoes and carrots were dished out to them. The stoical ones resigned themselves to feasting their eyes on Coporal Gates, since their stomachs would have to go hungry.

Maxwell was talking to his flight commanders. "I'm leaving both Webb and Cunningham with you, Jumper. I think it's a good idea to keep them together."

Lee looked towards the two newly blooded pilots, who were supine in deck chairs with their eyes shut; they had given up the study of aircraft silhouettes. He remembered what his tarty, sharp-tongued girl friend had said. There was nothing like that about either of these; the C.O. had got it right: they had spent months together surviving the strangeness of the first days of Service fife, the anxieties about being failed before they got their wings, and they counted on each other's reassurance. It was natural and healthy. They had seen their friend Gifford come and go within a space of two or three hours that morning. It must have scared the pants off both the poor little devils. Anything that helped them to keep their nerve was good.

He walked over to talk to them. "Nigel, you fly Number Two with me on the next detail… Stick like glue, right? Roddy, you're with Peter… Don't rely on Number Three to watch your tail – he's got his own problems… Never forget it takes four seconds to shoot down an aircraft… so look behind you every three…"

The usual macabre pleasantries, which provoked the usual polite half-hearted laugh.

He picked up a *Daily Mirror*: quick glance at Jane, in pants and bra for some unlikely reason; and Reilly ffoul, the wicked squire, thwarted, exclaiming "Stap me!" He couldn't know it then, but, two decades hence, these and Vera Lynn, the strip cartoon characters so innocent in comparison with what would amuse future generations, and the unashamed sentimentality of "We'll Meet Again" and "The White Cliffs Of Dover", would be as clear in retrospect as the headlong rush across the sky with guns blazing or the killing and the bursting bombs, as much a part of these days as the fighting and the hardships. The crassness of Reilly ffoul and the naive titillation of Jane would be as significant a war memory as the battles.

Knight sat between Harmon and Massey, with Moonshine's jaw resting on his knee, stroking his dog's ears with one hand and holding a sandwich in the other. Moonshine's eyes followed the sandwich every time his master took a mouthful. "Blackmail," Knight growled, and gave him half his bread and ham.

The three of them had been silent for some minutes. At first in a mild stupor after the rigours of the morning. Then in admiration of Cpl. Gates's contours. And finally in a hurry to finish their lunch before the next scramble.

Harmon broke the silence. "Swarms of the bastards."

Where?" Six-gun sat forward with a jerk. Knight incautiously let his hand fall and instantly lost another sandwich to Moonshine.

"I was thinkin' about's mornin'. Loverly."

"Jeeze, Bernie, I wish you wouldn't do things like that: I thought they'd crep' up on us."

"Gruesome little sod." Knight said severely.

"Yeah, what's lovely about it?"

"The way they're burnin' up flyin' hours they soon won't 'ave any left: no kites, no hours. No pilots, neither, at this rate."

Bernie had killed six Germans already that day and wounded two complete bomber crews.

"That's a hell of a way to figure it. Me, I'd as soon they stayed home, in the bloody *Vaterland*, or whatever."

"You're not keen, that's your trouble."

"You can say that again."

"You can't miss, they're such bloody swarms of 'em. Doesn't that make you 'appy?"

"If you knock off any more, Bernie, they're going to have to lengthen your fuselage to get 'em all on."

"Them bloody erks! All they think about 'ow many d'you get this time? Come back with a few 'oles and they think it's Christmas."

Blakeney-Smith had arrived to infest the scene. "That's called getting a vicarious thrill. Human nature. Can't blame the erks."

He had provided himself with an expensive air-mattress on which to take his ease, and now sprawled on this as though basking in the Riviera sunshine. It was only a question of time before someone on the squadron punctured it, and he must have known it, but such was his imperviousness to dislike or ridicule that he seemed openly to invite unfriendly acts by ostentatiously provoking them. Any day now he was likely to attach a large and impressively pedigreed dog to himself, merely to overshadow Knight and Moonshine. Perhaps his reason for not doing so was the knowledge that one of his comrades would surely feed the dog castor oil and lock it in its master's bedroom. Blakeney-Smith, who was as capable of self-deception as any schizophrenic could be, had no delusions about his popularity.

Dear God, he wondered, what made them so bloody impervious to the gut-freezing horror of incendiary bullets and the long, spinning fall to earth from thousands of feet high in an unnatural element? If God had intended men to fly he would have seen to it that they evolved with wings sprouting from their backs. They were hard types, most of them, with an enviable ability to suppress the horrors which must plague them as badly as they haunted him.

He had taken part in the destruction of two Heinkels that morning, following his leader in the attacks and holding his fire until he was close enough to be sure that he wouldn't miss. Since the start of this madness he had shot down two on his own, a Ju. 87 and a Me. 109. He was always afraid, but most of the time now he was able to overcome his fear. Yesterday he had not overcome it. He had baled out to escape from the fight Today he was ashamed of himself. Nobody would know it, because the sense of shame made him behave with more than his usual arrogance.

He had had pride and self-respect once, even though he had run away from school because he couldn't stand the incessant beatings; but perhaps that was as much from anger at injustice as from the pain. He had unflinchingly accepted all the other discomforts which were the privileges of an expensive British education: ordered to box for his house, he had used his fists toughly and not dared to back away; on the rugger field he had tackled hard, regardless of grazed skin and broken bones. Although he had taken up ski-ing because it was fashionable and costly, he had soon put his heart into it and earned the praise of instructors who didn't waste it on the unmanly.

But every test of courage demanded an effort from him, whereas his companions could apparently take them unhesitatingly.

He needed his drink. He needed his women. He needed his fast car. There was a fissure in his store of courage and resolution, and he had to make himself oblivious to it.

Anne Holt sat in a garden chair, tanning her limbs in a bathing suit. She had been out there all morning, with a pair of binoculars, listening and watching. Every time she heard a Hurricane she turned her field glasses towards it. Whatever the direction of the wind, and the fighters' take-off, they would pass over the house on their way to the Channel coast.

Sometimes they were too high for her to read their squadron markings, but if she could see those she could identify Peter Knight's individual letter.

She was a very pretty girl, with honey-blonde hair and big, lustrous blue eyes; four or five inches over five feet tall, graceful and full-busted. She played a useful game of tennis and had won good show jumping prizes. Boys had always run after her and men began to in her sixteenth year; at ski resorts they pursued her as though she were an adult. Now, at twenty, her conscience was uneasy: most of her girlfriends were in uniform, or nursing, or doing secretarial work in armament and aircraft factories. Her own contribution to the war effort was small: some work at the hospital, helping at a troops' canteen, and doing odd jobs at the air raid warden's post She knew it was a weak contribution, but joining one of the women's Services or training as a nurse would take her away from Peter.

Her father owned a light engineering company and had offered her a job for the duration; the factory was turning out components for aircraft, tanks, and armoured cars: but if she spent the whole of every day indoors she would not be able to keep an eye on the aerodrome.

She remembered all the young men from the R.A.F. station whom she had known who were now dead, wounded or prisoners of war, and lived in dread for Peter. As long as she had these long hours of freedom she could at least have some idea of his comings and goings.

He had been taking her out for four months, now, and she believed that their friendship would endure. At first she had wondered if she were making too much of it, but if she had had any doubts left they were dispelled by what he had told her the night before.

She had always enjoyed male company; sought it, like any other girl; been as ready to kiss and be friends as any ardent young man could wish. But although she fended off straying hands and turned aside invitations to bed, when Peter kissed her she longed for him to touch her breasts or put his hand between her thighs.

She knew that, if he didn't, it was not from innocence or lack of desire. Like every officers' mess, R.A.F. East Malford's had its regular peacetime camp followers: the mess tarts; gay, uninhibited girls of the easiest sort of virtue, who were invited to every party and dance and knew what was expected of them. When asked to spend a night in London or a week-end in Brighton they were delighted; if it was only a quick tumble on a picnic rug some Saturday afternoon, they were more than compliant.

They were the good sports, the pretty bits of crumpet, the generous sleepers-around who eventually married dull, solid citizens: consoled by memories of a few years of fun with wild young men who flew for a living and lived for the moment Some of them occasionally found husbands among these: no one held their past over-generosity against them.

Anne knew that Peter had taken his share of what was on offer. She was often more than a little resentful that he didn't shew more enterprise towards her. After all, those other girls had only liked him. Some of them may have been fond of him. But she loved him.

AN AIR BATTLE WAS SHOCKINGLY DIFFERENT FROM Webb's preconception.

For Cunningham, it was a breathtaking astonishment.

The first impact of combat passed in a flash and left both of them feeling completely abandoned. Neither of them had been prepared for the blinding speed at which everything would happen.

They had taken off in a state of some euphoria. When the scramble came they knew that they were about to be committed to the most frightening experience of their lives, but the sick tension passed immediately they were caught up in the helter-skelter rush for their cockpits.

The squadron was flying fifteen aircraft. Maxwell led, with Sergeant Wilkins as winger, while one of the other recent arrivals criss-crossed at the rear: weaver, arse-end Charlie. Webb, hugging Knight's starboard wing, with Dunal on the left, felt securely guarded. Ahead he could see Lee leading Cunningham and Blakeney-Smith. Behind him, in his mirror, were Poynter, Lotnikski and the other Pole, a sergeant; and Harmon with "Bishop' Viccar and Massey.

At the start all had been as he had anticipated; a few crisp orders from the section leaders and flight commanders; a lot of buffeting from other people's slipstreams and concentration on holding station; sweating preoccupation with engine revolutions, rate of climb, the precise position of his wingtip in relation to his leader. And the exhilaration that at last he was doing what he had joined the Air Force to do.

Then a lot of unanticipated events. First there was a burst of what sounded like machine-gun fire in his earphones and a voice said "Shut up, Bish," and he remembered that Viccar did impersonations.

Another voice piped up "Please sir, may I be excused?"

And from Massey: "You, Sister Anna, will carry the banner…"

All silenced by the GO.'s "Tighten it up, chaps. Turning starboard… Turning starboard… Go."

The silence broken by a grim "Here come the buggers."

Followed by Maxwell's unemotional "Number One attack… Number One attack… Go!"

Cunningham watched Jumper Lee slide down and to the left and followed him. Webb saw Knight break to the right in a downward-flowing curve and hared after him as the section re-formed from V into line astern.

They were both bewildered when they first saw their section leaders' guns firing; flame licking back over the wings, smoke trailing behind. Then they were in the smoke slicks themselves. Something was rattling against wings and fuselage. They didn't know what was happening. Each tried to follow his leader: they were flying into ejected cartridge cases and belt clips, metal hammering on cockpit canopy and engine cowling; they thought they were under fire and flinched. They held their thumbs ready over the firing buttons, but no sooner did a bomber flash into the sights than it was gone again. Another – and it was lost in a split second also. Where had the enemy gone? Why was aiming so difficult? This wasn't like shooting at a towed target, or even like camera gun dogfighting with an instructor. A gut-pulling turn, standing on the wingtip, the blood draining from the head, eyes going dim… greying out… a sudden blackout.

Recovery. An empty sky.

It had all taken less than two minutes.

Webb was drenched in sweat. He looked at his altimeter and was amazed to see that he had lost five thousand feet.

He felt giddy and confused. He had flown at 350 m.p.h. into the midst of more than a hundred aircraft. He had blacked out; and when his head cleared he was alone.

He remembered Lee's word: four seconds to get shot down; in panic he zig-zagged tightly and searched in his mirror for the fatal Hun In The Sun of the Air Ministry posters. There was nothing there.

He levelled out and looked around, looked down. A few aeroplanes weaved against a background of broken cloud. Above and on all sides vapour trails shredded away. Three or four miles away a fire burned in the sky and beyond it another. Far below, two parachutes caught the sun.

He felt the humiliation of failure. They would think him a fool or a coward for losing contact.

He tore round in a circle; a mile to the north there was another orbiting fighter. A Messerschmitt? He flew unhappily towards it with a lump in his throat and his heart thumping. The other pilot had turned head-on. How quickly everything happened. He began to count… when he reached ten, he would fire; his thumb was on the button.

It was another Hurricane and both altered course to pass within fifty feet of one another. Webb saw the letters on the other fuselage: Cunningham recognised him at the same instant and they flew home together.

Would this damned invasion never be launched? Richter mopped his face with a handkerchief and eased his damp collar away from his neck. What prevented the Navy and the Army from crossing that narrow strip of water? Why must they wait so irresolutely for the Luftwaffe to make it safe for them? They were all paid to fight and to take the same risks; why didn't the soldiers and sailors earn their pay, like the Luftwaffe had to? If they didn't care for the odds against them by daylight, they could invade at night.

He had had enough of this charade. Five times today they had escorted bombers on massive raids. Each time the Red Indians, the Hurricanes and Spitfires, had appeared from nowhere as though by magic. It was like a boar hunt in which the boars drove off the huntsmen. He thought it was a good, manly simile. He enjoyed boar hunting and admired the wild, vicious beasts he killed.

Would these mad Englishmen never give in? Were they bound in some suicide pact which kept them hurling themselves and their machines at each assault, out-numbered though they were? The Poles had fought bravely enough, but went under in five weeks. The British had held them off for months and shewed no sign of weakening.

He had lost three of his boys today. Helbig was dead: dear Franz with his springing ballet dancer's step and his fawn-like face with pointed ears and wicked eyes. A face full of invitation which had driven Richter insane with lust, although he knew that the invitation was not for the likes of him, but only for the girls who went so willingly to the young oberfeldwebel's bed.

His eyes lit on Keiling. Pathetically immature to be an officer, he thought. What thoughts lay behind those dreamy blue eyes, so large and long-lashed? What fears and doubts rioted in that head, under the tight flaxen curls? Here was a prize specimen of the Herrenvolk, with his milk-white skin tanned to a golden hue like the skin of an apricot, and with the same soft down; pale golden hairs on face and forearms.

Damn the British! They would not take this boy from him.

Then he thought: Damn we; I haven't spoken to him for twenty-four hours.

Oberleutnant Richter rose from his chair, causing a disturbance among his pilots, who automatically came to their feet. He called "Keiling! Come on, let's see if you can do better than yesterday." He turned to his second-in-command: "We'll stay in the circuit. If any orders come through, notify me at once by radio."

"Jawohl, Herr Oberleutnant." Leutnant Brendel, the stocky, hirsute deputy commander of the Staffel, saluted and wondered why the Old Man was taking so much trouble over this raw new member of the outfit. Evidently their losses were worrying him. In a pinch Richter trusted nobody but himself, rated no one's skill higher than his own. Brendel supposed that henceforth he would take most of the training of the new pilots into his own hands.

Hafner, who never seemed to tire or to lose his high spirits, voiced the thought that was in all their minds: "Can't be long now before we're released. How about a quick raid on the town?"

Ihlefeld yawned. "God! Erich. Not again tonight? I'm tired. Let's stay in the mess. We're on dawn readiness tomorrow."

"That's right," agreed Brendel "An early night for you boys: in bed by eleven. And I mean alone!"

"Puritan," scowled Hafner.

Pilot Officer Lotnikski had enjoyed his day. He did not care whether he lived or died. He had nothing to live for. He had lived twenty-five years in Poland; then, a year ago, came the barbarians to lay his country waste. They took from him everything he valued and left him only his life.

His father was killed in an air raid on Warsaw, his mother by German shells which fell on their country home. His elder brother died in an armoured car and his younger under the tracks of a German tank. His sister, nursing in an officers' hospital, had been thrown into a German military brothel and committed suicide. The girl he was engaged to had saved her life by betraying a Jewish friend to the Gestapo.

He hated the Germans as a nation and he hated them individually. They were the ultimate in corrupting influence, bestial behaviour and perversion of people's minds. He killed them emotionally, conscious of the slaughter in a different way from Bernie Harmon.

On some days the sorties he flew were only standing patrols but today every time he had gone up it had been because contact with the enemy was certain.

His combat reports reflected his attitude. Herrick, listening to him and setting down his words in better English than Lotnikski could muster, was worried; Lottie couldn't last at this pace. The man was crazy. The M.O. would have to do something; sedatives perhaps, for he knew advice would be wasted.

"I followed Blue Leader in an attack on a Do. 17, getting in two short bursts, the first from 150 yds, the second 50 yards. My leader had silenced the rear gunner and I fired into the port engine and cockpit. The e/a exploded directly beneath me and I was thrown on to my back. This made me lose visual contact with Blue Leader and Blue Three.

"I then made a full deflection attack on another Dornier, opening fire at 100 yds, and killed the pilot. Making a second attack, I hit the starboard engine. On my third attack I stopped this engine and the aircraft lost height. In order to preserve ammunition I made a dummy head-on attack, and the gunner or navigator who had evidently taken over the flying stalled and went into a spin from which he did not recover.

"On engaging three Me. 109s I used the last of my ammunition. I therefore broke off and was returning to base when I met a Heinkel making for France with one engine feathered. There was very little fire from its guns, so I knew that the crew were either dead or wounded or short of ammunition. I therefore flew alongside and edged in until my propeller was cutting into the fuselage. By this means I severed the tail unit and the aircraft immediately went into a steep dive and crashed near Dover."

Herrick's dry remark was "The Engineer Officer won't be pleased about damage to your prop, Lotty."

"That bloody plumber he has plenty more in the stores." Lotnikski dismissed all engineers and storekeepers with scorn.

He seemed to have formed a habit: for, later in the day, the I.O. wrote on his behalf "When the C.O. ordered us to make individual attacks I decided to save my ammunition for defence against 109s. I approached a Do. 17 from directly astern, fired a short burst at 50 yds, and killed the rear gunner. I then sliced through the e/a's fin and tail plane with my propellor. It went out of control and the three surviving crew baled out."

All his combat reports now contained such hair-raising statements as "I engaged four Me. 109s", "I held my fire until I was fifty feet below the e/a and fifty yards astern, whereupon I put a four-second burst directly into the bomb bay and the e/a blew up" "Having used all my ammunition and my engine having stopped and caught fire, due to earlier attack by 109s, I aimed my aircraft at the nearest Heinkel and baled out just before they collided."

Dunal fought with bitterness also, but to him the Germans were vermin rather than vandals. Many of his friends had been infected by admiration for the Fascists and Nazis: in contrast with the political instability and cynicism in France, at least these régimes seemed to have purpose and patriotism.

He flew with dash more than recklessness. He would like to survive the war and return to a new France and true civilisation.

More sensitive than his Polish comrade, he was a lean, fierce, lonely man, more cut off from the rest of the squadron than Lotnikski, because he was more fastidious.

At the end of a hard day of battle Lotnikski's face looked as crumpled and rough-textured as a convict's clothes; whereas the Frenchman's ascetic features, eyes red-rimmed from the strain of searching and sighting, wore the bleak expression of a suffering artist.

When he had taken the last of their combat reports, Herrick telephoned the Medical Officer: whatever could be done for them would have to be done with tact, but he knew he wouldn't sleep that night if he didn't do something about it.

THE CIVILIAN POPULATION OF EAST MALFORD CON-
trived to lead some social life despite the hard times.

Ernie Foster and his wife Marion were entertaining in their bungalow on the outskirts of the village.

Marion had taught in a girls' school until her marriage and was looked upon as an intellectual by her friends; she also sloshed oil paints heartily on to canvas and had an artistic reputation. Ernie had gone straight from school to the humdrum routine of an insurance office, where he now earned £400 a year. Ineffectual lawn tennis and even worse cricket were his contributions to the life of the community, with some inept amateur dramatics and work for the Conservative Association in the winter.

They lived smugly in a well-planned little home, where only an unexpected pregnancy would have upset their applecart. Their guests were two young married couples, both of whom had come on bicycles to save petrol Everyone was riding bicycles these days.

The two male visitors were fellow toilers in the City. One of them had conscientiously volunteered for each of the armed forces more than once, but been rejected on account of a heart murmur. He, like Foster, belonged to the Local Defence Volunteers, fore-runners of the Home Guard.

The other man was an architect who had actually been embod-ied in the R.A.F. for three months, as a member of the Volunteer Reserve, but released to a reserved occupation: he now designed military installations. He had not resisted when he was invited to leave the cockpit of his Hurricane for a drawing office.

There was plenty to eat and drink. The Fosters grew their own vegetables, kept poultry and made wine and beer. Their party was interrupted at midnight by a violent eruption of blinding light which leaped past the edge of the blackout curtains and was followed by a tremendous explosion, which rocked the bungalow and sent glasses flying. The front door rattled and a window shattered.

Amid screams of alarm from the young women, everyone rushed outside. The sky was lit by leaping flames against which a dense column of oily smoke climbed into the still air.

"My God!" Foster exclaimed indignantly. "A plane crash. It might have landed on us."

A voice from the night called roughly "Never you mind about that, mate. It's a bloody mile away. Nowhere near your perishin' 'ouse. And what about the pore sods inside it, eh?"

Marion uttered a yowl and groped for her husband's matchstick arm. Foster's indignant chunter was cut short by the owner of the rough voice, who appeared in the light falling from the open front door and revealed himself to be an air raid warden.

And close that door and drew them curtains. Wot yer tryin' ter do – shew 'Itler where to drop his bombs, then? You get them curtings drawn and that ruddy door shut, and look lively about it.

As Foster and his friends told the air raid warden shrilly, this was the sort of thing they were fighting against; Nazi hectoring. They would attend to the blackout in their own good time. Not only did trains not run to time, these days, but one couldn't do as one wished in one's own home.

"And," Marion added defiantly, "the glare from that burning aeroplane and all these fires where the Germans have dropped their bombs are *slightly* brighter than the forty watt bulb in our hall."

"Anyway," Foster told the warden, "it would be more to the point if you did something about these German spies who are all over the place, instead of persecuting British ratepayers about the blackout."

"Listen, mate…" the warden began aggressively.

"That's right," one of the guests cut in. "I heard only the other day about a man who was in a railway carriage with a nun; and when he looked down he saw she was wearing size twelve boots. Of course he called the guard, and some soldiers arrested the mm on the spot: and she turned out to be a man, a German spy who'd been dropped by parachute."

"I've heard the same thing," Marion agreed vehemently. "And they can prove a man's a spy who's been parachuted in, by taking his shirt off: there are the marks of the parachute harness on his chest and back."

"Don't you worry about all them rumours," retorted the bellicose warden. "They're getting as good as they gives: there's a Scotch regiment down the Isle o' Wight, see, and the Jocks don't like Jerries; they give all of 'em as bale out a taste of cold steel. Right in the guts. That'll teach 'em to drop spies in nun's clothes," he concluded with somewhat elusive logic.

He was interrupted by a scream from Marion. In the flickering glow from the burning aircraft she was a figure of stark accusation and warning, pointing a trembling finger down the road in horrified silence.

Turning to follow her direction, the others saw a tall man plodding towards them, wearing a flying helmet. His face was streaked with grime and blood and he swayed as he trudged up to the gate. He leaned on the gatepost and groaned "*Ich bin verwundet*... I... I... am... vound...wounded..." He swayed and fell to the ground.

There were shouts from the men and cries of alarm from their wives.

Foster ran inside and dashed out again wearing his L.D.V. armband and carrying a pre-1914 Martini-Henry rifle which he pointed uncertainly at the wounded German airman, who had by this time been hauled to his feet.

The warden pushed the muzzle aside. "Pack it in, mate. I reckon you're a lot more dangerous with that thing than what he is. Pore buggar." He took the dazed enemy by the arm and pulled him towards the front door. "Come on, you lot shut the door behind us then: look lively. Careful of the blackout."

"Oh, my God!" squealed Marion hysterically. "The blackout: after this!" Then, as it registered that the sanctity of her home was about to be invaded by the hated foe, she shouted "You're not bringing him into *my* house..."

"Oh yes, I am, Missus. And I'm going to telephone the Police and tell them to send a car to fetch 'im."

"I s-say," said Foster magnanimously, "get the chap a drink. After all, we can be civilised about this. Look at him: he's only a kid. Can't be more than twenty... Er... *Mein Herr*... er *wie viel jahre*... er... *haben sie?*"

The prisoner, who was on the point of collapse, appeared not to hear him.

The ex-R.A.F.V.R. pilot reminded the well-intentioned Foster sternly that his question was against the Geneva convention: rank, name and number only; asking his age was forbidden.

The warden startled them all by giving a loud and very vulgar guffaw.

"What," asked Marion frozenly, "do you find so amusing?"

"I was just thinking, Missus: why don't you take this young feller's shirt off and look for the marks of the parachute 'arness?" He had to release his prisoner and lean against the wall in a paroxysm of mirth.

The German, unsupported, crumpled at the knees and measured his length in the neat little hallway of the Fosters' bijou residence.

"Wizard! Really super controlling, Duffy." Knight, in an attire whose unmilitariness would have shocked the Luftwaffe, beamed at the duty controller.

Squadron Leader Duff, who had been a fighter pilot in 1914 -18, beamed back. He didn't even mind everyone in the Operations Room hearing this young junior officer address him so familiarly.

The girls around the plotting table and the two who sat with him on the dais overlooking it were watching Peter Knight with open admiration. There were several reasons for this. One was the basic mating urge: every W.A.A.F. tried to get herself invited out by a pilot; by an officer pilot if possible, and if not, by a sergeant. If aircrew ignored her she strove for a date with any officer. There was a scoring system in this highly competitive game.

Knight, jubilant, was a sight to draw any girl's eye as he stood on the controller's dais. He had come straight to the Ops Room from dispersals, after de-briefing by Herrick, to thank the controller personally for his indispensable help in shooting down an enemy aircraft at night for the first time.

There was a close relationship between the fighter pilots and their controllers, and any disparity of rank was ignored. Knight would never have dreamed of calling Sqdn. Ldr. Maxwell anything but "sir"; but Sqdn. Ldr. Duff was always "Duffy". It was a tacit acknowledgment of the fact that pilots fought while controllers stayed safely on the ground, and the former didn't have to respect anyone who was not risking his life.

Duff had a son the same age as Knight; a navigator in Bomber Command. He felt that he had a special affinity for young men like this. What a piratical, swashbuckling young devil this one looked. His turnout would have outraged the diehard, ex-Army, Royal Flying Corps senior officers of Duff's day; but in this war the lads wore whatever was practical and comfortable; and uniforms were expensive, not to be worn out thoughtlessly. They had to make some concessions to uniform: Knight, like most of them, confined it to an old tunic; with the top button undone after the new Fighter Command custom. That and a battered Service Dress cap with the stiffening taken out. His black flying boots and long white polo-necked jersey were R.A.F. stores issue, but looked more suitable for beagling than visiting the Ops Room. His grey flannel trousers, tucked into boots, shewed an oil stain or two and a patch over one knee where he had torn them climbing out of his cockpit.

"I kept losing him. And those ruddy searchlights: I wished I had my sunglasses. But it was a lot of fun. A change from day ops. No 109s around."

Duff listened with sympathy to the staccato comments. He remembered his own nervous condition twenty-odd years ago, when he used to bring his Bristol fighter safely back after a running battle with the enemy.

Peter Knight, he thought, was like a hefty, handsome young stallion. Unconsciously so. But the smiling girls recognised it: he wasn't shewing off up here on the dais, he was much too nice a type for that, but his stance and every movement were expressions of virility. One kind of excitement prompted another. Duff knew; he wasn't so old.

"The first I saw of him, Duffy, was his exhaust flames. He was about a mile ahead then. I opened the taps and crept up on him, a hundred feet below, so I could see him against cloud. Then a bloody searchlight came on and caught me instead of the Jerry. That really brassed me off, because the rear gunner spotted me at once and began shooting. I was up to within two hundred yards by then. And blind! I jinked a bit and presently the searchlight went out. I suppose you told 'em to. I'd been so dazzled that I couldn't see anything. That was when you gave me a couple of vectors and put me in contact again. But he nipped into cloud and I hung around, dunking I'd lost him, waiting for him to come out."

"That worried us, too," the controller told him. "There was another hostile around and another Hurricane chasing it. We thought the airspace was getting rather crowded."

"I'm glad you didn't tell me! Anyway, next time I saw him he was right in a searchlight cone. I went in to fifty yards before I opened fire. The rear gunner couldn't see me."

The scene came back clearly. It was only an hour old and still raw in Knight's memory. He had hesitated for a moment before jabbing the gun button. He was looking straight into the face of his enemy. The rear gunner, dazzled by the searchlights, couldn't see the Hurricane; but his eyes seemed to look directly into Knight's own. His face looked frightened and he seemed little more than a schoolboy. For the first time the war had become personal for Knight. His stomach muscles bunched and he felt ill for a few seconds. This was different from a whirling daylight battle with the sky full of aircraft. Then, all he ever saw was the shape of a helmeted head, the bulk of a body's outline. Now he was, it seemed, within touching distance and the German in the rear turret appeared as close as a man would be at the other end of the bar counter in the Mucky Duck.

He wanted to shew clemency. He had the illogical thought that if he fired a warning burst aimed away from the Heinkel the tail gunner would plead with his captain to land and surrender.

For ten seconds Knight prolonged the life of that German gunner. Then he killed him with a three-second burst from less than fifty yards.

He broke to the right and upwards, and turned in again. His target was corkscrewing violently, striving to evade the searchlight beams. He raked it with long bursts of accurate fire, shattering both engines and ripping away part of one wing.

He saw three survivors jump out and watched their parachutes open.

"Any news of the crew?" He asked Duff.

"Yes, as a matter of fact we've just had word. The pilot landed near the village: blundered into a bit of a party at someone's house. He's in hospital now, with a few broken bones and mild concussion. The other two were picked up on the far side of East Malford."

"I'll go over to the hospital in the morning and see how he's getting on. If he's fit enough, I might bring him back to the mess for a drink. It'll do the blighter good to see a spot of R.A.F. morale."

"You needn't think he'll write home and spread any pro-British propaganda, Peter!"

Anne sat up late, listening to the wireless and playing the gramophone. Listening also for the unsynchronised drone of German bomber engines. Knight had telephoned to say he couldn't leave camp that evening; she knew what it meant.

All evening there were intermittent take-offs from, and landings at, the airfield; but she knew this was only routine night flying training going on.

Faintly came the hum, now and then, of heavier aircraft high overhead. British bombers, she recognised, on exercises or making raids on Germany and occupied France. Not many of them: the R.A.F. was fighting a defensive battle just now; it was nearly all Fighter Command's show. Their party, as they called it.

Then it came. She couldn't explain to herself how it was, but she divined that this time the Hurricane she heard climbing away from East Malford had been despatched on an interception. The snarl of its engine sounded more vigorous than the others, as though it were in a greater hurry. It was climbing steeply too; she could tell that from the engine note and volume.

She was convinced it must be Peter. He wasn't the only pilot on night duty, but her anxiety and love drove her to this certainty.

The music played on and she did not heed it. She fidgeted Fetched herself a glass of cold milk from the kitchen refrigerator. Went stealthily out of doors to scan the sky, taking care neither to disturb the blackout nor wake cook. The maid lived in the village. Anne's parents had gone out to dine and play bridge.

She gazed at the sky and felt lonely. She wondered what she would do if a German parachuted on to their lawn. She was frightened of Germans. She had met any number of them in Austrian ski-ing resorts; big men, tall and heavily boned; masterful and loud. She had read newspaper stories (false as well as true, had she known it) of their atrocities all over conquered Europe.

Anti-aircraft guns were blazing away somewhere; she could see their flashes as well as hear their bombing. British fighter pilots, Peter among them, were up there in the black sky now, hunting the German bombers. Some of the enemy were bound to be shot down. Some of the crews would take to their parachutes. They had to land somewhere. Why not in East Malford? In the garden of her home?

And what about the invasion? Everyone said Hitler was ready to launch it at any moment. The Germans had thousands of paratroops: suppose they were to be the vanguard of an invasion? They would drop by night. They would land at places like East Malford, which had an R.A.F. airfield; and some of them would drift wide of their objective. She glanced fearfully around the shadowy two acres of lawns and shrubbery that surrounded the house.

She was about to hurry inside when a detonation like the crack of doom rolled over the down-lands and a pillar of flame-leaped into the night, towering in a flickering orange and yellow fury of conflagration high above the woods, the roofs and church tower; startling an owl from the tree by their drive gate, to fly hooting past her head. Sparks cascaded above the tips of the leaping flames and the earth trembled.

Her heart missed a beat and she choked for breath. Peter! No, it couldn't be: that ear-splitting thunder must be a bomb-load exploding.

She turned down the volume of the radiogram, doused the drawing-room lights and stood by the open french window to listen for the sound of a Hurricane's return. She had no way of distinguishing one Hurricane from another, but she had made up her mind that Peter had taken off; that he had destroyed that bomber; that he would land now.

She saw the red and green lights at its wing tips before she heard its engine. And then, incredibly, the lights began to draw a smear across the sky, rotating slowly. She blinked. There was no doubt about this: someone up there was doing a slow roll. A victory roll. Anne was no aviator and a slow roll at night meant nothing to her: she had no notion of the difficulties and dangers of aerobatics in the dark, with no horizon and no contrast between earth and sky.

A lot of people watching on the aerodrome, however, had a very fine appreciation of Peter Knight's skill.

" 'MORNING, KEILING. PREPARED FOR YOUR BAPTISM of fire?"

"Good morning, Herr Oberleutnant. Yes, Herr Oberleutnant."

"Good. But make sure it's not baptism by total immersion! No swimming in the Kanal."

The C.O. was damnably hearty this morning. Always a bad sign. Brendel glanced at him, then returned to his breakfast. Moody devil. You never knew what the Old Man would get up to when he was in this frame of mind. His trouble was an excess of courage. Brendel had won an Iron Cross too, but his supreme ambition was to become an ex-serviceman, not an inscription on the town war memorial. Richter was spoiling for a fight today; he knew the symptoms. Perhaps he was impatient to get this business over; there Brendel could agree with him. So, he knew, were all the others. What was the Army waiting for? Or was it the Navy who chicken-heartedly postponed an invasion, on account of unfavourable tides or some such nautical claptrap?

This phase of the war was dragging on too long. He hoped that today would bring a really good blitz to end it. What he wanted to see now was German war material on the beaches of Sussex and Kent; and it had better be soon.

It was too damned early for breakfast. He couldn't stomach more than a couple of cups of coffee spiked with cognac.

He noticed that few of the others touched any food. Many of them were helping themselves from the brandy bottle. The C.O.

preferred hot milk and red wine: it looked like a child's soft drink, pink in colour. A real boar-hunter's pre-dawn start to the day, Richter claimed: he was too damned jovial by half, this morning.

Brendel knew that his Staffel Commander's mood could, and probably would, change mercurially. He was buoyant at the moment but it wouldn't take much to plunge him into gloom or, worse, anger.

The pilots filed out to the cars waiting to take them to the airfield.

"Come with me, young Keiling. And you, Erich; sit in front with my driver: Keiling and I will loll in the back like pashas. Eh, Manfred?"

Keiling was no less startled than Hafner at the use of his Christian name. Even his junior comrades hadn't called him by it yet. He knew he would have to wait for acceptance until he had a few missions under his belt. The C.O.'s kindness made him feel uncomfortable.

"May I bring Wolf with me, sir?" asked Hafner.

"Hell! I'd forgotten about your damned dog. Yes, let him sit in front with you. But make sure he doesn't leave any hairs on *my* trouser legs."

With sudden spitefulness, Hafner, looking at Keiling, announced casually: "I used to keep a rabbit called Manfred. I named him after von Richtofen. I was a very air-minded boy. I hoped it would give my rabbit some courage. He grew into a huge buck and the terror of all my friends' does."

Richter laughed loudly. "Hear that, Manfred? Are you a buck, Leutnant Keiling? Do the little doe-*mädchen* tremble for you?"

The boy was blushing and silent.

There were tents around the makeshift aerodrome, to provide somewhere for the pilots and ground crews to rest and have their meals when on duty. One of them was a field office where the adjutant and the C.O. did some of their administrative work. It was too early to bother with files and memoranda; Richter went down the line of aircraft with his Engineer Officer and a group of mechanics and armourers, pausing now and again to take a closer look at some repair or modification that one of them pointed out. This done, he sat among his pilots in their tent, watching a game of cards and furtively stealing glances at Keiling's beautiful young profile.

Presently their first orders came and he went to the blackboard which stood on one side of the high-walled tent and drew diagrams while he briefed them for the day's first raid on England. "We are going to knock out an important fighter station south of London," he announced with relish.

Dawn brought release for East Malford's duty night pilots.

Knight eschewed the smelly brown blankets that were provided in the crew room and used his own sleeping bag. He woke, as he always did, to a hand rocking his shoulder. But the touch was diffident and the face that grinned at him expressed plain admiration. In place of his batman it was his rigger who had brought him a mug of tea.

He crawled out of his sleeping bag, drove back to the mess to shower and shave, and telephoned Anne.

"Did I wake you up?"

"Of course not. You aren't the only one who gets up early."

"I don't from choice."

"I thought you were going to get some sleep this morning?"

"Don't need any. Had plenty last night. Anne..."

"Yes?"

"I love you just as much today."

"Oh, darling. Listen, where were you when that German plane crashed near here last night?"

"Where were *you*?"

"In the garden…"

"That's no place in an air raid," he said severely. And added swiftly: "Whom were you with?"

She laughed at him. "An owl. It came out of its tree like a rocket when the plane exploded."

"Anyway, you shouldn't wander about out of doors when there's an air raid warning: you could easily get pranged by a chunk of shrapnel from an ack-ack shell, or a bomb splinter. You ought to know that."

"Don't be so crusty. I only went outside because I thought I'd hear you better coming back."

"How did you know I wasn't in my sack, fast asleep?"

"Intuition."

"Intu-my foot. You stay inside another time."

"You were up, though, weren't you?"

"Actually… yes."

"Did you see the plane crash?"

"Yes. I had quite a good view of it."

"You shot it down!" she sounded excited.

"What's this: more intuition?"

"Then you did!"

"I would have told you, if you'd let me get a word in edge-ways."

"Pig," she said happily. "I'm so proud of you. Wait a minute…" He heard her calling her mother. A moment later she went on "Mummy says congratulations and will you come to dinner tonight? She's putting a bottle of bubbly in the fridge for you."

"Thank her very much."

"Now go and get some rest. And I love you. Terribly."

Rest would have to wait. Knight went to ask his Squadron Commander for permission to invite the German to the mess.

Sqdn. Ldr. Maxwell, chewing his pipe, said "All right, Peter, if you want to. Fetch him this evening." He was thinking about the first German he had shot down, in France, nearly a year ago; a gunner in a Do. 17, in which the rest of the crew had died. He had visited him in hospital and the occasion had not been a success. The wounded air gunner was rude and angry. It was not a meeting of chivalrous foes who had fought a good, clean fight and were now ready to shake hands. The German hated him for what he had done to his friends, who had died horribly: one torn to pieces by Maxwell's bullets, the others in flames, trapped in the wreckage.

Maxwell recalled how he had gone from the hospital to the nearest church, although he wasn't a Catholic, and tried to pray for the three dead men: that hadn't been a success either.

He felt that Peter Knight was wasting his time, but he had better find that out for himself.

Fit. Sgt. Viccar and Six-gun Massey, who had also been on night readiness, went with him.

"How are we going to talk to this bloke?" The Bishop wanted to know. "D"you speak German, Pete?"

Knight spoke a roughly understandable German, with slashing ungrammatical fluency and aplomb. "I did four years of it at school, and I spent a couple of holidays in Austria and Germany, but that was a long time ago. I can get by. But he'll probably speak English."

Each of them was wondering what it would be like to confront a specimen of the Master Race. The enemy was always the impersonal occupant of an aeroplane, and now they were going to see him in the flesh, harmlessly grounded.

Knight was beginning to think that he would have done better not to suggest this jaunt. The Jerry would probably think they'd come to gloat. Was there a touch of condescension in the visit; the victor patronising the vanquished? Would the hospital staff think he had come to shew himself off? And if this German was like so many others he had met, arrogant and defiant, he would feel a great fool in front of his friends.

Massey was curious to take a close look at captive Superman, something to write and tell the folks in Corpus Christi, Texas, about. He was fighting for something he believed in, against something he detested: now it would be embodied.

Viccar had a professional desire to assay for himself the quality of a German airman. He had been impressed by the German Air Force's success in Poland, France and the Low Countries. He often asked himself whether there were some perceptible rare quality in these German air crews. A guardsman was instantly recognisable among other soldiers. Perhaps the Luftwaffe had the same kind of distinction: it would be interesting to see for himself.

A group of nurses waited to welcome the three of them. They had been on duty all night, but this was a chance not to be missed: it wasn't every day that three front-line pilots came by. Viccar, swarthy and saturnine, jauntily mo mustached, made a date with the prettiest of them.

The doctor who took them to the patient's room treated them with the deference he usually reserved for consultants.

"How is he?" asked Knight.

"He had rather a bad biff on the head, a broken ankle, a broken arm and three broken ribs. How he managed to walk at all, let alone as far as he did, I don't know. He must have a lot of guts."

Knight felt guilty, "Was he wounded, Doc?"

"A bullet through the forearm, that's all; it didn't do any permanent damage."

"I must be a lousy shot: I was aiming at his engines."

"He caused quite a stir, turning up on somebody's doorstep in East Malford."

"So I hear. What's his name?"

"Leutnant Kurt von Hippel."

"Does he speak English?"

"Quite well, the nurses tell me. As it happens, I did some post-graduate work in Heidelberg, so we talk German."

The doctor opened the door and Knight hesitated.

Massey gave him a push. "Go ahead, Pete. Don't be chicken." The tall young German lay with one arm bandaged and the other in a cast. A bruised swelling on his forehead was partly hidden by sticking plaster over a stitched cut.

He stared straight ahead, ignoring the four men and the nurse who accompanied them.

Viccar and Massey looked expectantly at Knight He cleared his throat and said "*Guten Morgen Leutnant von Hippel. Wie geht es Ihnen?*"

The head on the pillow turned and the grey eyes in the pale face looked into Knight's, reminding him of the way the rear gunner had seemed to look straight at him before he had killed him.

"*Ziemlich gut, danke.*" The German's voice was steady and dispassionate.

"*Und Sie sprechen Englisch sehr gut, nicht wahr?*"

"*Ein wenig.*"

"That's good. We can get along faster, and my friends can understand."

"Please, not to speak too fast."

"How do you feel?" Knight repeated, wishing he could be more original.

"How would *you* feel?"

"That's a good question," Knight said lightly. "Looking at the pretty muses around here, I think I'd feel rather pleased."

The nurse standing on the other side of the bed chuckled.

"We have pretty nurses in Germany also."

"I'm sure you have. You've got a lot of pretty girls: I've been there."

For the first time von Hippel shewed interest. "So, you know Germany?"

"Not well. I've done a bit of ski-ing in Bavaria."

"My home is…" The German cut himself off. Name, rank and number only.

"Are you in much pain, Herr Leutnant?"

"No thank you, Herr Flying Officer. You see, I am knowing your rank."

"Well done. Is there anything we can do for you, or bring you?"

"There is no need, thank you. I will be home in Germany soon."

This was too much for Massey. "Someone's been fooling you: we're not planning to exchange any prisoners."

Von Hippel scowled. "So, America is in the war? You are not declaring war, but you fight secretly for the English. Such honour-ableness." He turned his head away.

The three R.A.F. pilots exchanged glances. This was what their reason had warned them to expect from a captured Nazi, yet when they encountered it the reality was as surprising as though they were unprepared. None of them had a suitable reservoir of words on which to draw. They were all articulate men, but for the moment they were silenced by the scorn and insolence of a wounded man whose philosophy they despised. It was ridiculous; but all of them felt, in his own way, in the wrong.

Massey at last broke the silence. We're free people. That's some-thing you wouldn't understand. An American is free to volunteer for the R.A.F. and the British are free to take him or refuse him." Then he felt his own anger mounting and his voice rose, hardening. "It's a *personal* matter: I happen to hate you Nazi sons of bitches worse than I hate rattlesnakes; so I came here to fight you; because I *want* to. When did you last do something you *wanted*, to and not just because that cruddy Führer of yours *told* you to? We're free human beings, here, not machines or puppets..."

The German remained staring at the wall, seemingly ignoring him. Knight interrupted Massey. "Forget it, Six-gun. He knows, without you telling him."

Still not looking at them, von Hippel said "Herr Flying Officer, I think the American a false argument makes."

"He is not arguing," Viccar said. "He's bloody telling you, mate."

Knight said "I think it would be better if we change the subject: after all, we have you at something of a disadvantage." The German thought about this, putting the words together in his mind. Then he turned and faced Knight.

"You are a gentleman. I would like to know your name." Knight told him.

The German nodded stiffly. Knight thought that he must be clicking his heels too, under the blankets. "I will use my influence for you when we occupy England."

There was a spontaneous roar of laughter from the nurse, the doctor and the three pilots. Frozen-faced, angry, von Hippel tried to stare them down, but they rocked with successive gusts of laughter, the tears coming to their eyes.

Von Hippel, his fists beating on the coverlet as best they could, his face reddening, shouted "When we occupy England, for all who have helped me I will my best do."

"We'll hold you to that," Knight told him, through his mirth. "We are coming. You cannot stop us."

"We could debate that all day, but I'm afraid the doctor wouldn't allow it." Their laughter had stopped now. "We hope you do come: because stop you we certainly can. And will."

"You will see."

"We didn't come here to quarrel with you, Leutnant von Hippel. Our Commanding Officer sent us to invite you to visit our mess. We would have liked to entertain you this evening. Unfortunately…" He gestured an indication of the wounded man's injuries. "We didn't know, you see."

The German pilot's eyes filled with tears and he looked away quickly. They saw his Adam's apple working as he swallowed hard. Then he said "Excuse me. I am still… shock… shocked, *jah*? You understand? I thank you. My apologies to your Commanding Officer. I regret I am unable to accept. Thank you for coming to see me." He turned his back to them.

The doctor touched Knight on the arm and they all filed out. Knight was the last to leave and heard his name spoken quietly. He looked back. The German had turned to face the door and looked directly at him. His right arm was raised and for a moment Knight wondered whether he was expected to shake hands. Then von Hippel sketched a salute and said "Good luck. As we say, *Hals und Beinbruch*."

May you break your neck and your leg. The traditional German pilots' way of saying good luck, from the First World War: because it was bad luck to say "good luck"; and good luck to offer wry wishes for disaster.

Knight smiled at his enemy. "For you, it has already come true. I hope you will be comfortable."

"We will meet again," von Hippel called after him as Knight walked away. "And next time, you will be my guest: in your own mess, my friend."

Before they left the hospital Knight gave the doctor twelve and six. "Please take this and see he gets a bottle of Scotch. That'll be O.K., won't it?"

"Unofficially. All right, I'll see he gets it."

"Thanks. With my compliments."

"If you insist. I don't think he deserves it. But it's up to you."

"He's not a bad type. Nothing wrong with him that a spell in prison camp won't put right."

Driving away, Massey commented "A sad sack. A real sad sack. Poor guy."

"Yes, he'd have been a bit of a damper if he had been fit enough to come to the mess."

Then they went to bed for the rest of the morning and when they reported back to dispersals Blakeney-Smith told them "You picked a good time to have your morning off; four scrambles already."

"Tedious," they said; and "Time you earned your pay, Simon"; and "You need the practice; we don't" Blakeney-Smith got no change out of them.

The squadron took its ease in canvas chairs on the grass in the murmuring summer afternoon, with insects buzzing and skimming over the grass, the thud of a cricket ball on a bat coming from somewhere near the workshop hut, Moonshine snoring and occasionally whimpering as he chased cats in his dreams.

Cunningham and Webb sat with their chairs close together. Their eyes were shut but sleep evaded them.

Knight leaned towards Bernie Harmon and asked quietly: "How are the new boys doing?"

"Not bad, Pete. They bagged a Dornier between them and claimed a Heinkel."

"They're learning fast. Sticking together?"

"Yeah. Just as well. Neither knows enough on his own: the two of 'em together just about make one fairly competent fighter pilot."

Knight had to laugh. You cynical bastard, Bernie."

"What's wrong? They're alive to prove it, aren't they?"

There was no counter to that.

Maxwell, from under half-closed lids, was observant, as always. He had heard what they had said. He remembered Bernie Harmon before this frail boy had acquired his unshakeable attitude of self-reliant competence. He was quick-witted, dangerous, a maker of swift military decisions which were always the right ones; or had always been right so far. Webb and Cunningham would acquire some of the same abilities in the coming weeks. For the time being there was a blundering uncertainty about their actions in the air; but he himself, their flight commanders and their section leaders must remember that they were vulnerable and needed help, protection, teaching.

When Webb and Cunningham had acquired this instinct their hold on life would become a great deal less tenuous.

Meanwhile the day wore on and scramble orders came again and again. Boys who had dates with their sweethearts that evening died two or three hours before the trysting time. Young men who had promised their wives that they would be home early to supper ate their evening meal in hospital or a prison cell, or not at all.

"Well, that wasn't so bad, eh, Manfred?"

Oberleutnant Richter had always admired under-statement. Traditionally it was a characteristic attributed to the British. He saw no harm in admitting good qualities in the enemy. A little reserve was certainly better than histrionics.

The boy Keiling looked pallid after his hard day. His face was smeared with oil and cordite: he had touched one of his gun ports

inadvertently and then put his hand to his cheek. He was thinking to himself that he had had as near a glimpse of hell as he ever
wished to have, and if this was what aerial warfare was always like
he was already sorry he had joined. He could not hope to live
long through such a holocaust. As long as he was being nursed,
as the Staffel's newest fledgling, he might hope to survive. But
how quickly could he learn to rely on himself? In a day or two he
would no longer be the rawest of neophytes. Replacement pilots
would be coming in. They would have to be nursed in their turn;
at his expense.

He had learned one terrible lesson on that first day: it was
the least experienced pilots who died first. In his innocence he
had supposed that the longer you were in a Staffel the greater the
odds on your turn coming next to be shot down. He had quickly
realised that it was exactly the contrary. The old stagers lived on.
The new comrades went down in flames.

And now here was this huge, broad-shouldered, athletic,
fearless Staffel Commander saying "It wasn't bad". Yet, despite
his heartiness, he was kindly and avuncular as well. One had to
respond to him; as much from genuine fondness as from respect
and discipline.

Keiling forced himself to smile. "Not so bad, Herr
Oberleutnant. But I know I was lucky. I was well looked after."

"I am glad you recognise that, Manfred. But survival is not
all a matter of luck and protection. Those are the least parts of it.
Essentially, your fate is in your own hands. You did well today."

The boy flushed happily. He pulled himself up and snapped
his heels together. "Thank you, sir."

"Good. Well, let's not hang about. Time we went back to the
mess and cleaned up. And we deserve a drink." Richter, slapping
his flying gloves into his open palm, added "Come on, I'll give
you a lift." A thought came to him: obvious favouritism would

be foolish. He called across to Brendel: "Come along, Rolf, I'm waiting for you."

His deputy commander hurried over and the three of them strode towards the staff car, the youngest man walking a step or two behind the others.

Keiling was in deep thought. A mental roll-call. Schmidt... Bekker... Pelz. Three youngsters like himself; all newcomers to the Staffel during the past two weeks: and all killed or wounded today. The two who had survived were badly hurt. Being shot down and wounded, or injured in a crash landing, was not like getting a rifle bullet through you if you were an infantryman. It meant, usually, lumps torn from your body; the bones of your legs, arms or back shattered; burns on your face and hands. He had seen dead men dragged out of crashed aircraft when he was at flying school; there was never one who had not been smashed, mashed, pulped, incinerated. And this was worse: if that could happen to you through your own ineptitude, how much more terrible were the things that a Spitfire or a Hurricane could do to you with its guns.

And then he remembered that he had weapons too, just as potent as the enemy's; and he could batter and pulp them just as horribly as they could hurt him.

He was still wondering whether this knowledge was any real satisfaction when they drew up at the farmhouse.

"Out you get," said Richter cheerfully. "We'll see you later in the mess."

Keiling stood rigidly at the salute, watching the car disappear.

A fight van stopped nearby. A huge dog bounded out and gambolled around him. He relaxed, smiled and fondled Wolf's head.

The dog's master, jumping down from the van, remarked "He likes you, Manfred. He is very discriminating; not everyone receives such a compliment."

"I like all dogs, Erich." Keiling recalled Hafner's sarcasm about his name and the pet rabbit. It seemed to have been a remark made in another life, long ago. Since then he had lived through many deaths and suffered the most appalling fear he had ever experienced.

Everyone was tired, but everyone had a bottle of cognac in his room. Hafner flung himself into a chair and Greiner put a glass in his hand, then bent to put slippers on his feet. He hovered attentively, waiting for his officer to break the silence.

Presently Hafner said dreamily: "Greiner, have you ever had a hate fixation?"

The batman started. "A hate fixation, Herr Leutnant? What is that?"

"Have you ever fixed your general hatred for any group of people on one person, so that he becomes symbolic of the whole group? That is what I am asking."

"Oh, yes, Herr Leutnant. When I was a young man I used to play football for the club in my town. I hated the team from Riedlingen, our greatest rivals. And I focused my hatred on their centre forward. He scored most of their goals. I was the goal-keeper you see. Year after year the Riedlingen club beat us. And year after year I came to hate that centre-forward with all my heart. Is that what you mean?"

"A very good example, Greiner. That is exactly what I mean. So you will understand my hate-fixation: it is for a certain Englishman…" Greiner raised his eyebrows in astonishment. "He is a Hurricane pilot and I see him often. I know the letters on his aeroplane: YZ-E. And he has a silly, puerile decoration on the nose: a stupid caricature of a mongrel dog chewing a bone; and the bone is shaped like a swastika." Hafner thrust out his glass and the batman refilled it. "He is arrogant and insulting; and childish. His attitude is typical of the feeble, distorted British sense of humour. One day soon I am going to shoot him down. I will kill him. I will make sure of that. For me, this has become a personal matter."

Mildly, Greiner said "I did not know that you hated them so much, Herr Leutnant."

"Hate? I don't hate them. I despise them; they are naive and foolish to defy us. I have been to their country. They were friendly; but that is the well-known British duplicity. Still, I do not hate them. I did not hate the Poles. I hate the French…" He broke off and his eyes twinkled. "Not the girls; only degenerate Frenchmen. Germany and France have always hated each other. But the English, that is different. We fight them, but only because they interfere: they fight us because we justifiably made war on Poland and France. We do not need to hate them to fight them hard. But I do hate this one particular English pilot."

Hafner nourished his hatred on more brandy and the wine he drank at dinner. Later in the evening his personal vendetta against the anonymous Englishman became mellower; but no less virulent. Now he was able to regard it as an act of special distinction to single out an opponent for personal combat. That was the way they did things in 1914-18. That was the Richtofen-Udet-Göring tradition. He would perpetuate it; and the man whom he had chosen for his victim was destined only to play a part: there was nothing personal in his enmity. It was just the other fellow's bad luck for having the poor taste to decorate his Hurricane in that derisive manner. And the Englishman was too successful in combat too; all those crosses to flaunt his victories.

Richter saw Keiling coming towards him to say good-night formally before leaving the mess.

He rose as the boy came up. "I know you like good music, Manfred. Come up to my room for a nightcap; I keep a very special old brandy; and I have some records: Wagner and Beethoven."

They mounted the stairs together. The Staffel Commander's room was big and luxurious, with a private bathroom and an excess of florid furniture. They sat sipping cognac and listening to German music until the younger man fell asleep. Richter roused him gently and sent him to his own quarters.

Richter stayed awake for nearly another hour, tortured by doubt. Had he fallen in love or was it just that he lusted after this beautiful young male?

Was it mere deprivation, frustration of his desire, that drove him towards Manfred Keiling? If he could take a short leave and find himself a boy in Paris or Lille; some sailors' queen in Calais; best of all, get himself to Berlin for forty-eight hours and have his choice of the most vicious youths in Europe: then would he come back purged of his longing to possess Manfred? Or would his desire persist? If so, it must surely be love. Perhaps he ought to put it to the test. But how could he leave the Staffel now, even for forty-eight hours? He knew he could not.

He must stay. Stay near Manfred, forcibly. What happened in consequence was beyond him to prevent.

During the afternoon three more scrambles had been ordered. Each time, 172 Sqdn made contact with the enemy. Each time, Pilot Officers Cunningham and Webb won a little more of the experience that would help to keep them alive; if only for the next sortie.

Every time the telephone orderly yelled his message they exchanged a look of brief agony before they took to their heels, pelting for their aircraft in a fine frenzy which may have given the illusion of an aggressive spirit but was more a desperate urge to get the terrifying business over and done with.

Since their first operation they had grown progressively, and rapidly, less confused. Events happened still with bewildering speed, but both knew what to expect and were better prepared to retain some coherence of thought.

Although they flew in separate sections they usually came together after the formation had broken up. Being alone was horrifying. Webb reefed his Hurricane into tight spirals whenever he had lost his leader or been lost by the others, searching for another Hurricane with which he could join. That was his conscious intention. Sub-consciously he was looking for the letter "K" which would identify his friend. Cunningham, when isolated, climbed in tight circles looking for Webb's "N".

Four times out of six they had flown home together. On the other two, both had climbed far above the battle height and hared for base with plenty of ammunition left; then wasted time orbiting somewhere out of sight until they could decently land not too long before the rest. Each of them felt ashamed when he had given way to his fear.

Connie Gates was in the Officers' Mess lobby when 172 trooped in that evening. She saw how wilted the two youngest and newest of their pilots were and was filled with protective compassion; and more: for they were handsome boys, both of them. They both had fair hair and apple cheeks which the sunshine out at dispersals had tanned; when they left the mess this morning they looked healthy and fit. Now look at the poor little devils, she thought. "Little" was entirely an endearment, for both stood several inches taller than she.

A pint will soon make them feel better; and the other boys are good to them: all that joking and horseplay, the high spirits. They'll buck up soon enough, she told herself.

But she kept her eye on them.

She knew the losses that all three of the squadrons had suffered during the day. News travelled fast from dispersals.

Later, Connie saw Peter Knight leave the mess in his best blue, freshly showered. You'd think he'd just come from a game of football or cricket, she thought: he looked pleased and as though he had exerted himself, but no more. This was how her husband and his friends used to look when they came in to tea after a Saturday afternoon match; bruised, perhaps, and shining clean from soap and hot water, content with their strenuous efforts and with a long, pleasant evening to look forward to. She knew he was off to see that nice girl of his. She approved of Peter; and his American friend.

Knight was embarrassed by his reception. Anne was waiting for him on the porch and Mr and Mrs Holt made a fuss of him.

Anne's father had served at the front in the previous war. With Knight he was sometimes almost apologetic, as though the money he made by turning out parts for aircraft and armoured vehicles were dishonourably gained. Even if he were young enough, he would not have been allowed to join in this war: but he commanded a Home Guard company and talked to Knight about firearms and the defence of his factory. Knight knew little about weapons except those with which aircraft were armed, and didn't care much either, but like any other young suitor was a willing victim of his girl's parents' obsessions.

Mrs Holt, who was smart, pretty and sometimes a little silly, especially about good-looking young officers, gave him a few bad moments. But Knight wasn't one of the best objects for her bright chatter. He wasn't a pretty boy, and he manifestly didn't need petting or mothering.

They dined well. The Holts were able to keep a good table although the nation was on short commons. They reared pigs and poultry, had a kitchen garden and an orchard. The promised champagne, before dinner, and a decent burgundy with it, caused Knight to reflect on the advantages of being a successful industrialist compared with the lot of a busy general practitioner like his own father, whose meals were usually hurried and often inter-rupted. He made the comparison in no mood of criticism. The Holts were always good to him.

He was enjoying himself, but at heart felt uneasy away from the squadron. Here, he missed that elliptical, instant, often tele-pathic communication he had with the men who shared his most esoteric experience; among whom a phrase was enough to express more than he could, to the uninitiated, with long explanations.

The past few weeks had isolated him even more among his immediate comrades. His life was in their hands and theirs in his. He realised it, but did not dwell on it. As soon as he politely could, he took Anne away.

The "Mucky Duck" was, as usual, crowded. Someone was trying to push past him and he looked around. A busty little woman with gipsy hair and long earrings gave him a tipsy smile.

"Can you let us squeeze up to the bar? We're shela-celabrating: my husband captured a German parachutist lash… last night."

The conversation in their corner of the room died suddenly. Heads turned, and Maxwell, catching Knight's eye, raised his eyebrows.

"A p-parachutist?" Knight repeated.

"Well, actually a German pilot." Marion Foster amended.

"What an exciting life you lead. Do tell us more."

Foster chipped in: "He was the pilot of the Heinkel that crashed near our house last night Damned nearly took our roof off…"

"Only another mile nearer and he would have," Blakeney-Smith said loudly and unkindly.

"…I can't really claim that I captured him…"

"Yes, you did, Ernie." Marion was having no modest disclaim-ers from her husband.

"…I don't think he could have gone another step. He sort of surrendered, really…"

Later on, Blakeney-Smith nudged Knight and pointed towards Webb and Cunningham who were swaying slightly, flushed with heat and beer.

"The Theban pair, slightly pissed."

"What?" Knight was impatient with the interruption.

"The Theban pair. Don't you know your Greek history, Pete?"

"Obviously not well enough."

"Let me enlighten you. The Theban Army was lousy with homosexuals, who fought in pairs. Plato – you have heard of *him* presumably? – and a handful of them could defeat a regiment, because they shewed such devotion to protecting each other…"

"Belt up, Simon," Knight said disgustedly.

"…The first time the Thebans were beaten, three hundred pairs were found dead, all with frontal wounds; they may have been ready enough to turn their backs on each other, but not on the enemy! I reckon our two over there are a typical Theban pair."

"Don't be a bastard, Simon. Do you always have to give us the full nausea?"

AUGUST CAME AND SIX OF THE TWENTY PILOTS ON 172 Squadron were replacements for those who had gone during the past three weeks.

Every day started with at least one squadron on dawn readiness and ended at dusk for all but the night operational pilots at readiness. The day's end found them tired to the marrow of their bones.

But weariness did not send them all early to bed. Many seemed to need frenetic amusement night after night, to distract them from the catastrophes of each. day. Every evening saw two or three crowded cars roar away from the mess to London, packed with officers and sergeants from all the East Malford squadrons. There was never a night when the mess bar closed before midnight, and every night boisterous games of rugger, high cockalorum, "Are You There, Moriarty?" and polo (played with chairs, wooden spoons and that increasing rarity, an orange) raged until even later. Making the circuit of the ante room without touching the floor was another popular and not undangerous diversion.

Very few could keep up this hectic relaxation without an early night now and again, but there were even fewer who never took part in it at all. Perhaps it was because they had discharged an excess of adrenalin into their systems that these young men seemed so inexhaustible, or perhaps it was the alcohol which kept them going. It may have been just youth, abundant health and the effervescent energy bestowed by unfailing high spirits. Between scrambles most of them fell asleep.

No one mourned and no one spoke of the dead. They talked about their battles, with much weaving of hands to shew what this and that aircraft had done; they laughed abundantly and ridiculed each other. The most macabre incidents caused the greatest amusement. A predicament which could result in someone's death was watched by his comrades with ribaldry.

These incidents, providing light relief of the R.A.F.'s peculiar variety, were part of the fabric of those days. It was a time of change and adaptation. Commanders of other squadrons came on brief visits, to exchange experiences and views on tactics. Some squadrons occasionally experimented with sections of four instead of three, the newly-named "finger four" formation, so called because the leader flew with one man behind and on one side, and two echeloned on the other; the formation thus resembled the four fingertips of a hand. Another new idea was to operate in pairs, the wing man never parting from his leader whatever happened.

Air fighting was becoming more brutal as well as more sophisticated. Until now, most of the R.A.F. had believed that war in the air was a chivalrous, impersonal form of combat; unlike the sordid slogging match between infantry and artillery. Airmen understood one another's problems, as they fought to the death, and admitted some admiration, even if more or less grudging, for the skill of their opponents. This was an illusion which quickly crumbled in the intensity of that summer conflict.

Inevitably fighting became bad tempered and bitter. The strain on airmen was first aggravated by the stupidity and over-eagerness of their own side. It was a common experience for British fighter pilots, parachuting to hoped-for safety, to be challenged, often fired at, by the Home Guard, who mistook them for Germans. Some of the R.A.F were wounded by these too-enthusiastic amateur warriors. Farmers pointed their shotguns and threatened, assuming that anyone who had come down from a battle overhead must be an enemy. It was bad enough for the British, who could quite soon convince the most sceptical uniformed civilian or minatory armed peasant of their identity by employing suitably well-chosen Anglo-Saxon expletives. But for the Poles, Frenchmen, Dutch and Belgians, whose foreign accents were baffling and unconvincing, the risk of death at the hands of those whom they were defending was always present in this situation.

There were other manifestations of bestial stupidity. Knight was shot down one afternoon and as he parachuted towards a meadow he could see some strange activity: a dozen yokels were prancing round a haystack, waving their arms and performing a travesty of the goose step. They all carried pitchforks, rakes, scythes or billhooks. As they saw him coming down they paused; then, evidently satisfied that he was a friend, continued their procession. He could hear them chanting, drunkenly, "We'll Hang Out The Washing On The Siegfried Line"; and concluded, correctly, that they had drunk rather a lot of strong beer in the hot sunshine at their lunch break.

When he had released himself from his parachute and stood up, he saw the body of a German airman lying near the haystack, with a parachute dumped near it.

He was sickened to see that the leader of the capering parade carried the German's severed head on a pitchfork. Another farm-hand, immediately behind, flourished the scythe with which he had decapitated him.

They were grinning at Knight, inviting his approbation. He rushed at them, punching and swearing. He knocked down the leader, who dropped the pitchfork, sending the head rolling grotesquely into some nettles. He knocked out the man with the scythe and was tussling with a third, before the rest fell on him and, with drunken jibes, thrust him, still struggling, into a lorry. As he was driven away he saw the German's head affixed once more to the pitchfork and the gala resumed. They bundled him out at an anti-aircraft site and he went from there to a Police station; but nobody seemed to want to believe him when he told them what he had seen ordinary, decent Sussex farm workers doing.

When he reported to Herrick, the latter, with a face of doom, said "You'd better hear what Six-gun has to say."

"What the hell has he got to do with it?"

"Ask him."

Knight turned to Massey. "What happened?"

"Christ, you wouldn't believe it. You saw me shot down…"

"I believe that!"

"I baled out and landed in a field right next to a wood where two guys from a Ju. 87 had come down. Two soldiers came running out of the wood, with rifles, and one of them said "It's O.K., sir, we've done for the bastards." I asked them what in hell they were talking about and they just pointed to the trees and took off. I went in there and found two Jerries; one with his head bashed in and the other bayoneted."

Angry and ashamed, Knight could only stand in silence. Presently he said "If word of this kind of thing gets back to the Jerries, it's going to be rough on us if we have to bale out over there."

II JG 97 had suffered as badly as 172 Squadron.

Baumbach, Weber and many others were dead. The chairs in which they had sat at the mess table stood in front of empty places which the new arrivals left alone.

The Staffel had lost several pilots from wounds or bums; others were now prisoners in England.

Mealtimes were dour and silent and there was a lot of heavy drinking. The pilots drank in their bedrooms, in the mess, and in the bars of Calais and Boulogne. They brought girls back to bed and went at them like blood-crazed Goths.

Keiling had started to bite his nails. Even the squat, unimaginative Brendel, Richter's second in command, had developed an uncontrollable jerk of the head, as though he were perpetually scanning the sky for enemy fighters.

The Staffel Commander was never far from the handsome young Keiling. In the evening, unless summoned by the Gruppe Commander to drunken, fornicating revelry in the chateau, he invited the boy to his quarters, where they sat in silence, listening to gramophone music.

Hafner had developed a dichotomic attitude towards his aircraft. It was an obedient, sensitive instrument in his hands, the means of self-protection; he respected and admired it, and there was no elation to equal the freedom of soaring above the clouds in a clear sky, diving, rolling, looping, and flying his Me. 109 to its limits. But it was also the hated weapon which took him into danger. When he saw it every morning in the dawn light he loathed it. Presently it would be his duty to climb into that narrow shell and take it far into the dangerous air that the enemy held. As long as it was serviceable he was its slave. When he turned his back on it at the end of another day survived, he was satiated with fear and sadness. He had seen his comrades shot down and German bombers disintegrated in cataclysmic explosions; heard bullets on his own armour plating and whistling through his wings and cockpit. His fighter with the wolf's head offering defiance to the enemy was the symbol of his fear and sorrow and his heart was cold towards it. But when he was on his way home victorious, he was joyous and he loved it with greater warmth than he had ever felt for a girl.

He came back from a mission one morning and walked across to Ihlefeld, his closest friend, who had landed earlier, took him by the arm and led him away from the others. "My God, Otto," he said in a low, shaking voice, "what sort of war is this? What's happening to us? We're behaving like animals, not like men with a code of honour."

"What's upset you, Erich?"

"Man, I couldn't believe my eyes. I had to go right down to deck level to get away from two Spitfires that were chasing me. I had no ammo. left and God knows where my Number Two had lost himself. I was making a tight turn to try to shake them off, when one of them grazed a tree on top of a hummock, and crashed. I saw the pilot get out, unhurt." He paused and shook his head in disbelief. "Another 109 appeared from nowhere and gave him a burst. The poor swine was blasted right off his feet, flung ten metres up in the air… riddled. Is that necessary? If a man gets away with it, good luck to him; he's out of the fight until he gets in an aeroplane again and can shoot back. But shooting a pilot on the ground… that's sheer viciousness. It's murder."

Ihlefeld put his arm about Hafner's shoulders. "I know how you feel old boy. I wasn't going to say anything about this, because it's bad for morale; but I'll tell you, now. I saw one of ours shooting up a Tommy who'd baled out, yesterday. The poor devil was drifting down at two thousand metres, when this brave comrade of ours lined him up in his sights and let him have it; right through the body; he just burst apart. I don't mind telling you, I nearly puked."

"God! I'm not surprised. Did anyone else see it?"

"Must have."

"Hell! We can expect the same from the Tommies, then. What a damned idiotic thing to do."

Cunningham and his friend Webb had just shot down a Do. 17 between them. As the crew were scrambling out the bomber exploded, killing them all. Cunningham felt as though he had been reborn, so great was his delight: the exhultation of victory had made him great with glee, and now this dramatic thunderburst of sound and bright colours filled him with ecstasy. Why the hell should they get away with it? Look what they were doing to England with their bombs.

He yelled at Webb on the radio, some incoherent phrase that startled the other: he saw him turn and raise a hand in acknowledgement.

Webb was a few yards in front of him and they raced together into the heart of the bomber formation again. The dogfighting developed in its usual pattern: a sprawl all over the sky, bunches of aircraft suddenly breaking up, scattering, melting away.

There came a moment when a Hurricane, in flames, dropped ahead of them in an inverted spin. They both saw the pilot fall clear and his canopy open. An Me. 109 instantly opened fire and shot away the parachute, sending the British pilot down to a cruel end, with many seconds in which to contemplate it.

It was Webb this time who screamed some incomprehensible message over the R/T. His voice choked off suddenly and Cunningham knew that, like himself, he was heaving up the contents of his stomach. There was a foul smell of vomit in his oxygen mask and he impatiently unfastened it and pushed it aside, then wiped his face with his sleeve.

They saw two more parachutes and heeled over in a tight turn towards them. These they would protect. Then they saw that the men attached to the parachutes were both Germans.

Webb pulled away, but Cunningham drove deliberately at the nearer of the enemy airmen and carried away his shroud lines with his wingtip. He saw the German's face turned to him, screaming. He banked and made for the other parachute and destroyed it also in the same way.

Then he began to tremble so much that his hands on the control column made the Hurricane wallow and his feet set it yawing.

What had he done? What had he become in those few moments? Everything that he believed in had deserted him. All the principles that had been bred into him had vanished in an instant. He retched again and again. A slimy mess dribbled down his chin. His Mae West and shirt were fouled. The gaudy scarf around his neck stank of filth. He began to blubber.

He forgot that he had to fly this aeroplane. He let it take him wherever it would. And then he felt the pressure of "G" crushing him, his head rolling wildly, and found himself in a steep corkscrew dive. He jerked himself back to immediacy, pulled the stick back and blacked out. His hand moved on the throttle, the aircraft lurched. He came back to full consciousness whirling around in a spin. He straightened out, wiped his eyes and looked wildly around.

A stream of tracer tore past overhead and his eyes turned in shock to the mirror. A Hurricane just behind him was rocking its wings. It dived past and Webb waved at him to follow.

When they landed, Cunningham sat in his cockpit for a minute or two, resting his head on his arms. His rigger, standing on the wing, leaning over the cockpit, was full of solicitude. "Air sick, sir? Come on out of it, then; we'll soon clean it up. I'll get some water for you to wash before you go to the crew room."

When he clambered down to the ground, Webb was waiting for him. "Sorry to scare you, but I thought you'd gone to sleep. I fired over your head to wake you up."

Cunningham said nothing and they walked in silence towards Herrick.

Neither of them mentioned the two Germans.

That night they both got reeling drunk; for the first time in their lives. Webb blamed himself because his friend was drinking himself into a stupor. He knew that it was because Cunningham was filled with remorse; he had been on the brink of killing the two parachuting airmen himself, and felt now that he had been disloyal to a comrade in letting him do it on his own and carry the whole burden of guilt.

Early in the morning Knight and Sgt. Wilkins were scrambled to intercept an unidentified aircraft. They caught up with it over the Channel; a Junkers 88. They shot it down.

As they crossed the Kent coast on their way home, antiaircraft batteries opened fire.

Knight broke left. Wilkins broke right and a shell hit him square amidships. Knight heard the explosion and turned hard to look for his wing man. All he could see was a billow of smoke, out of which fluttered a few scarcely recognisable pieces of Hurricane.

He yelled into his microphone, reporting the guns' mistake to the Operations Room. His first intention was to tempt the battery to identify by firing at him. He'd shew the bloody fools: he'd go down and blast them out of their snug sandbagged emplacements.

The controller's voice came calmly, ordering him to return to base immediately. He must have shouted some unguarded threat in his rage. He ignored the controller and dived to ground level, streaking out to sea again. He knew where some of the gun positions were in this area, and deliberately made three passes shooting at the first three he saw. Even if none of these had fired at Wilkins and him, they would soon spread the word to their trigger-happy chums. And if he were accused of a grave breach of discipline, he would claim that he had been firing at a low-flying enemy aircraft which the gunners had failed to spot.

On mid-morning the war struck for the first time at the very heart of R.A.F. East Malford.

All the deaths and injuries of the weeks gone by had been shared by everyone and the sense of involvement was complete.

But, however harrowing and sad, the killing and the wounding and the capturing had been experienced at second hand.

First hand involvement in the battle came when, one bright morning, eighteen Ju. 87 Stukas dive-bombed the station, fifteen Heinkels dropped their high explosives and incendiaries from ten thousand feet, and Me. 109s swarmed in to strafe with machine-gun and cannon fire.

Warning of the approaching raid came too late. The radar stations detected large enemy formations approaching the coast, but had no indication of their target. It was only when some of the raiders altered course that the Group Controller deduced that East Malford was the objective. Most of the other R.A.F. stations in the south had been attacked recently and East Malford's turn was long overdue.

Eighty-two Squadron were already airborne, scrambled to intercept the raid when it first appeared on the radar screens. Now, urgent scramble orders were given to 172 and 699.

Pilots rushed towards every available aircraft, whether it was on the operational roster or a reserve. The twelve men who had been detailed to fly on the next sortie had their own aeroplanes to run to; in addition, there were eight or ten pilots and four or five Hurricanes spare on each squadron. The most alert of the pilots beat their comrades in the race and left them, disappointed, to take shelter in slit trenches.

Knight, pelting at full stretch towards "E" was overtaken by Blakeney-Smith. He saw Cunningham stumble and fall, and Webb trip over him; but both were up in a trice and in full stride again.

The air was reverberating with the thunder of hastily started Merlin engines. Dust flew from the propeller wash.

Knight, looking to his left, saw an airman stagger as he ran forward, doubled over, to pull the chocks away from Webb's aircraft. The man put out his arms to save himself, then automatically straightened. The tip of Webb's propeller blade sliced through him, carving his head, shoulder and one arm from his body. A fountain of blood gushed into the air and the mutilated corpse collapsed.

Knight felt a stab of pity for the youngster in the other Hurricane's cockpit. He switched on his transmitter and called urgently "Roddy! Don't hang around. Get cracking, man. Get cracking." As he gunned his own machine away he saw Webb move jokingly forward.

Hurricanes were racing across the field, taking off up-wind, down-wind and across wind. There was a brilliant flash as two met almost head on and fused in a tangle of metal. Smoke and flames were followed by an explosion.

More incandescent bursts of flame, eruptions of smoke, scattered clods of earth, as bombs fell.

Maxwell saw Blakeney-Smith's Hurricane soar into the air before any of the others. He himself was close behind. He sped after the attackers, opening fire on a Stuka at extreme range as soon as it came into his sights.

Harmon muttered angrily to himself as he clawed for height with the throttle pushed through the gate; he hated to torture machinery, and his engine was not yet warm enough to take these high revolutions without damage. He cursed the bombers and picked one off at the moment it was about to release its load: it disappeared in a pall of smoke and metal shards.

Massey, who had been delayed by an engine that wouldn't start, looked down and saw Dunal leaving the ground only a hundred feet beneath him. A bomb exploded ten yards from the Frenchman. He saw Dunal's Hurricane flung onto its back.

A second later it ploughed in and buried itself deep in the turf, burning.

Knight, climbing fast towards the slanting dive-bombers, saw first one hangar and then another hit by high explosives and incendiaries. A roof caved in. Massive girders and pillars bent like twigs. Sparks and flames cascaded high into the shimmering air. Whorls and scarves of smoke eddied and swelled. A petrol bowser caught fire with dazzling intensity. Burning oil sent dense, rank, plumes of black smoke aloft. There were shell holes all over the green surface of the aerodrome. A crater on the parade ground. A shuddering tongue of flame leaping out of a partly demolished barrack block.

Maxwell and his men flew like maniacs, everyone on his own, no thought of joining up in pairs: every man for himself, now, and driven by a bitter resentment; killing was their daily task, the risk of death was their daily lot; but why involve the others, who, taken by surprise, could not even get as far as an underground shelter or a trench? The ground defence gunners were pumping Bofors shells and Browning bullets into the air. Someone hit a Me. 109 as it flew low across the middle of the airfield, strafing the dispersal huts. It lurched on to a wingtip and cartwheeled to destruction. But others followed it, blasting men from their lightly protected gun posts.

Knight, as he climbed away hunting a Stuka, saw a well known adversary flash past on his way down to attack a row of petrol bowsers: he glimpsed the snarling, slavering wolf's head with its blood-dripping fangs. He saw the pilot twist his head up and round, in recognition, and for an instant he was tempted to wing over and follow him down, pumping bullets into his cockpit; but he knew that by the time he turned and dived the other would be gone. Besides, it was the bombers which mattered most.

He wondered if any stray bombs had fallen near Anne's home.

When she took the lunches round that day, Connie Gates remembered what she had learned in school about the greatest catastrophes of history. None of them could have been more horrible than this: either in the event or the aftermath.

A stench of charred flesh, burned oil and cold ashes hung over the whole station. Two lop-sided hangars, a crumbled barrack building and several smashed steel and wooden huts were charred and scarred, amid the Fire Section's pools of water. Hoses still coiled around roads and buildings. The skeletons of lorries and burned-out petrol bowsers littered the tarmac bordering the airfield. Men hurried about with stretchers. N.C.O.s bawled at salvage squads moving at the double with picks, spades and barrows. Everyone was in haste, clearing up the mess, seeking the injured, removing the dead.

The surface of the aerodrome was torn up and pitted, but there was room for the Hurricanes to land if they took great care.

At 172's dispersal the ground crews toiled in silence to make their charges ready for the next mission. The pilots sat mute in deck chairs, while the Intelligence Officer went round to each in turn asking quiet questions, noting the subdued answers.

Connie almost cried out when she saw the two who were her particular concern. They scarcely looked like the boys she had known for the last few weeks. Their shoulders sagged, their faces were haggard and dirty. Their usually neat hair was tousled, their clothes were awry. Both looked glum and grief stricken; and scared.

She paused for her usual few seconds to gather everyone's attention, but few eyes turned in her direction.

She noticed that Bernie Harmon was lying back with his eyes shut while his fingers beat an incessant tattoo on his knees. Spike Poynter shifted his shoulders compulsively from side to side, wriggling as though his chair were infested by ants. Lottie was staring into space, dead ahead, holding a long, silent conversation with himself, his lips moving distortedly, one fist thumping his thigh. She knew that men under strain developed these uncontrollable tics. She had seen survivors of torpedoed merchant ships brought ashore in her home town, still twitching after their ordeal. It wrung her heart to see these young men, who had so bravely undergone so much, so stubbornly resisted any weakening of spirit, lose control of their nerves.

When she had been right round the perimeter road and the van was empty she saw a muscular figure, stripped to the waist but wearing a steel helmet at a jaunty angle, wielding a spade vigorously. There was something familiar about this apparition, this embodiment of earnest toil. She said to the driver: "Stop a minute, will you. I want to see if this is who I think it is."

"Aw, c'mon, Corp., I want me dinner…"

"Stop, I said: I won't be a minute."

The van came to a halt alongside the brawny man with the spade. A sweat-streaked face turned and scowled at her, then broke into a grin.

"Hello, Connie. Come to give me a 'and?"

She chuckled. "You're doing all right on your own, Norm. Here…" She delved into the rear of the vehicle. "I've got a drop of coffee left over." She poured him a cup and Tuttle paused to take it with a broad wink and a nod of thanks.

Driving on, she thought: First time I've seen our Norm Tuttle doing an honest job of work. Had to encourage him.

HAFNER JUMPED DOWN FROM HIS COCKPIT, A HAPPY man. What a feast of destruction that was! He had enjoyed every minute of the sortie: the joining up with the other escorting fighters, the circling while they waited for the bombers to arrive at the rendezvous. It had given him a sensation of safety and tremendous strength, to be part of, and to see, such a swarm of German aircraft.

He had fought one short engagement with a Spitfire, obviously flown by a novice: he had caught him unawares and shot him down with two quick bursts. Then had come the heady indulgence in an orgy of destruction which left him as elated as though he were drunk on champagne. It had been unimaginable excitement to see his bullets and shells ripping through a Hurricane which was standing outside a hangar, with a group of men around it; they had been tumbled like wooden soldiers swept aside with a sweep of the arm. He had shouted with joy as his fire tore into wooden buildings and poured through the windows of a barrack block.

He had only one regret: for an instant he saw his specially-hated enemy, the Hurricane with an "E" next to the roundel, and the dog tearing up a swastika stencilled on its nose. They had passed in a split second and there was no time to turn and go after it.

It was the start of a busy day that brought him as much pain and anger as that initial delight.

In a fight over the Channel he saw a Me. 109 shot down by another: in that crowded air space, with bullets and shells as thick as hail, one of their own fighters flew straight into the fire of another.

Coming back, he got into a fight with a pair of Spitfires which were attacking a Dornier whose starboard engine was smoking and letting off a stream of sparks.

The Spitfires alternately attacked the bomber and tried to drive Hafner off. Eventually the Dornier flopped into the sea a few yards from the Sussex beach and the Spitfires, obviously out of ammunition, disappeared. Hafner, making one last orbit to ensure that there was no lurking danger, saw one of the German bomber's crew climb on to the wing and turn to help one of his comrades out. But before he could do so he flung up his arms and pitched into the sea. On the beach knelt two British soldiers with rifles at their shoulders. A second crewman appeared and they shot him too. Two Spitfires came rocketing out of nowhere and Hafner had to climb frantically away.

He was like a hungry hunting animal that has been thwarted of its prey, as he walked stiffly away from his aeroplane. If only he could have fired one short burst at those two kneeling figures on the sand. His shock at what he had seen the day before was replaced by an even greater revulsion for the coldly calculated murders he had witnessed on that English beach. That was not war. Not only was it a violation of the Geneva convention, it was a crime against decency.

He did not remind himself that perhaps those soldiers had seen their own parachuting airmen murdered by Messerschmitt pilots.

Keiling was standing alone in a strange attitude, like a dummy taken from a shop window and placed here amid all this activity. Where everyone else was animated, the boy stood rigidly, isolated as much mentally as physically.

Hafner paused in passing, but one look at that distorted face was enough to change his mind. Whatever was torturing the boy, breaking into his privacy would not make it any easier to bear.

Keiling felt like a criminal. He had been tempted to delay his landing until he was down to his last drop of petrol, so as to put off as long as possible the moment when he must meet his comrades' scorn. But then he had thought it better to face the situation and get done with it. And now they were all ignoring him.

It was the sun shining directly into his eyes which had dazzled him and led to his mistake. But that excuse did not ease his torment.

He had been badly frightened during that battle when the British fighters were coming at him from every angle. He had been convinced that everyone of them had singled him out as its target. To begin with, it was demoralising to find the Spitfires and Hurricanes always waiting for them, despite the bomber attacks on the English radiolocation towers. It was uncanny and made his flesh creep. Never once did they catch the R.A.F. napping.

On top of that, a dozen R.A.F. fighters proved capable, time and time again, of doing as much damage as one would expect from sixty. True, the odds were up to five to one against them, and they had to fly and fight to even the score by sheer skill and bravery. But that did not account for their terrifying ubiquity, their unhesitating attacks on big German formations which, whether they stolidly maintained position or broke up and scattered, came off second best.

With the sun flashing on so many perspex canopies, with so many gun and cannon muzzles alight with flame and smoke, with so much turbulent air created by the swift rush of aircraft and the explosion of petrol tanks and bombs in their bays, Keiling felt confused and trapped.

So many bright surfaces reflecting the brilliant sunshine of the high, clear atmosphere. So many darting, weaving, shooting aircraft to dodge.

He had glimpsed one in his mirror and whipped round so tightly that he blacked out. Vision returned and he saw a fighter diving, it seemed directly at him. His eyes were still unsure from the effects of a tight turn, and the sun dazzled him. He opened fire and the diving fighter soared straight up as though a giant boot had kicked it in the belly. It stalled, fell on to its back and spun past him, the pilot dead. He saw then that he had destroyed one of his own side.

Could his mistake have gone unseen? In that milling crowd of aircraft, surely someone must have witnessed his mistake?

When he landed he had expected to be surrounded at once by angry comrades; to be marched in front of the C.O. who could be very different from the kindly music-lover with whom he shared his evenings.

But nobody had taken any notice of him. This was worse even than being ridiculed and villified: ostracism was the most hurtful punishment of all. He could not force himself to mingle with the others. He saw Hafner approach, hesitate and go on. Brendel came by, glanced at him and passed in silence.

It was the middle-aged, fatherly Intelligence Officer who broke into his shell. "What's the matter, Manfred? Not feeling well?"

In a choking voice, Keiling said "I didn't mean to… it was a mistake…"

The older man laid a hand on his arm. "I don't know what you're talking about, son. Come and sit down in the shade and tell me all about it."

Together, talking quietly, the two of them moved away. When Keiling's confession was over, the I.O. held him with a direct gaze from behind his thick glasses. "Forget about it, my boy. It's not going in the combat report. You can't be certain. No one else "saw a thing. That machine was probably hit by a Red Indian you didn't even see."

How childish it was to call enemy fighters Red Indians, Keiling thought petulantly. But what did it matter? What counted was the fact that no one had witnessed his disgrace; and the I.O. would respect his honesty and reveal nothing.

In two weeks the attitudes of 172 Sqdn and II JG 97 changed from dispassionate enmity to angry hatred. Weariness, especially when it robs men of appetite, creates a mood of sullen misery which maintains a smouldering resentment, erupting into spasms of willing brutality.

Both Germans and British were tired of the incessant strain of flying and fighting. Pilots, whether they wore R.A.F. blue or Luftwaffe grey, spent the hours of waiting with their stomachs quivering and their thoughts full of horrific images. But the periods of waiting were too short: hardly would they land from one sortie than they were despatched on another. They stumbled from their cockpits and flung themselves down on the grass, in the shadow of wing or fuselage, and slept. If they slept they had nightmares. If they stayed awake they had day-dreams.

Whether missions followed in quick succession or at long intervals, the burden was equally heavy. To land, refuel, rearm and climb back into the cockpit left little time for dark thoughts. To lie on the grass or loll in a chair, wooing sleep which wouldn't come, was hard on the nerves; and nervous exhaustion soon created intense physical fatigue.

And who could face food when his nerves and muscles were both worn to their limits, when his friends were dying or being wounded every day and most of his thoughts were about the moment when his own turn would come?

There even came a surfeit when drink was spurned. When last night's wine or beer, brandy or whisky, had left one's stomach and mouth so sour that the very thought of any more was revolting.

The bombers, with their escorting Me. 109s, came back to East Malford in the afternoon, only four or five hours after their first raid; and this time the spirit of some of those who had taken a severe bombardment that morning, and had no weapons with which to fight back, broke.

The R.A.F.'s ground defence gunners stood fast in their pits and their emplacements; those, at least, which had been repaired. Many of them died over their Brownings and Bofors and Hispano cannon. But some of the officers and men who could do nothing more than run for shelter and hide until the thunderous, flaming onslaught was over, could not face again the darkness of narrow underground shelters too like the grave, or the scanty protection of shallow trenches, while the earth quaked under the concussion of bombs and fire streaked across the ground in the wake of streams of petrol. When debris blocked the exit from a shelter, the roof caved in, or a river of flaming aircraft fuel and oil poured down the steps, any other place seemed preferable.

When the enemy attacked that afternoon, there was a stampede. British airmen and their officers pelted for the camp gates, dignity and example forgotten, all sense of self-respect gone in the helter-skelter rush to get away from the target area, from the tomb-like shelters, and find safety above ground in the surrounding fields and woods.

Those who stood firm tried to bar the paths of the fugitives, but were knocked down and trampled on. Service policemen at the gate drew their revolvers, but hesitated, not knowing what to do. A few of them fired warning shots into the air, which were ignored. Overtaken by an event for which they were unprepared, they had no precedent or training, no realistic instructions, to guide their actions. It is one thing to ordain this and that drastic measure in the face of panic, mutiny or mob violence; quite another to put it into practice, especially against one's comrades.

Tuttle, still labouring with his spade to repair the damage of the morning, was over-run by twenty or thirty men with two officers among them, scurrying towards the station main gate. Knocked down as bodies cannoned into him from behind, he picked himself up, swearing, and lashed out with the flat of his spade. Laying about him, he cracked three or four heads, and as his victims rolled on the ground he stood over them, his legs spread, his big muscles standing out under the sweaty sheen of his grime-streaked skin. With the edge of his spade ready, he yelled abuse at them, threatening to cut off their heads, their limbs, to emasculate them, if they did not at once turn back. For a moment, as the bombs and bullets rained down, he was tempted to run after the fleeing mob, but some shred of pride sustained him and he shook his fist at the Heinkels high overhead before herding the men he had tumbled towards an air raid shelter.

Several thousand feet above the fighting, Simon Blakeney-Smith circled in his Hurricane, keeping well away from that devil's cauldron of massed air power, the dense curtains of shell and bullet, the wily Messerschmitt pilots who hunted in couples and fours and outnumbered the British fighters so many times over. His body was sticky with the sweat of fear, his hands heavy on stick and throttle, his mind fogged by loss of willpower and fear of the unknown. He could not make himself go down and join in.

Bernie Harmon was in the thick of it. Lotnikski had tagged on to him and together they made a death-dealing, almost unescapable combination. Both men had learned to attack with such speed and accuracy that they could sight, fire and break away in half of the time that was necessary for the common run of fighter pilots. Of the two, Harmon had the advantage: he was the better shot and the more masterly pilot; but there was very little between them. What shade the Pole lacked in marksmanship and flying technique he made up for in self-sacrifice: he was like a human projectile, using himself as unsparingly as he used his machine and his ammunition to destroy the enemy. It was all the same to him whether he brought down a 109 or a Heinkel with bullets, his propeller, or by ramming it as a last resort and killing himself at the same time. Teamed with Harmon, he knew that he had a partner as savage and brave as himself. But Bernie wanted to live and he didn't. Or at least, he didn't care one way or the other.

Harmon cared very much. He thrust thoughts of Sarah out of his mind, for fear of weakening; and then he decided that he had better not banish her from his thoughts, because she was the reason for his determination to stay alive. Lotnikski, if he had let his mind wander, could have filled it with recollection of the endless stream of willing girls, in and out of uniform, who came to his bed; and went from it to someone else's. But they were mere pastimes, not replacements for the one he had lost.

II JG 97'S MESS WAS QUIET THAT NIGHT. THERE WERE more empty chairs at the dinner table, more toasts drunk during the meal.

The tired men sat listlessly sipping brandy, smoking and talking in subdued voices. The exultation of a few weeks ago was replaced by sadness over friends who were missing. Victory in an air fight was no longer a novelty; but even if they had felt like celebrating, how could one decently, when a friend who had shared a joke at lunch time was now nothing but charred flesh or limbless pulp?

Hafner sat with Wolf's chin resting on his knee. Ihlefeld put a record on the battered portable gramophone; a moment later a sentimental popular tune filled the room.

Richter was grateful for the excuse this offered him. He stood up, bringing all his officers to their feet. He smiled at Keiling. "Come on, Manfred, let's go and listen to some real music; and a decent gramophone." He paused. "Anyone else interested?" Nobody accepted his invitation. He made a perfunctory Nazi salute, muttered "Heil Hitler" and went out, followed by his young *protégé*.

Keiling was feeling as though his bowels had been scraped with a blunt chisel. His throat and mouth were sore from retching in the privacy of his room, with only a sympathetic batman as witness, and the brandy he had drunk before and after dinner. He could not get over the guilt of killing one of his own comrades. He could not rid himself of his fear that any day now he would meet his match in the air: every time he flew it seemed to him that the British were becoming more expert, more savage. In his mind were clear pictures of every German aircraft he had seen shot down during the day, yet he could hardly remember seeing German victories.

He followed his Commanding Officer into the now familiar room with its four-poster bed, the curtains around it inviting seclusion from the worries and dangers of the life outside these cosy draperies, these homely walls.

"Make yourself comfortable, Manfred." Richter smilingly gestured to a deep chair. The boy sank into it, his eyes following the older man's movements. He was beginning to feel powerless to think or act for himself. His life was in Richter's hands. As long as Richter was there to protect him, to care about him, he was cocooned in strong armour. He could feel the affection flowing towards him, just as he felt the sturdy presence when they flew wingtip-to-wingtip.

A low voice said, "Here's your cognac." He looked up, straight into Richter's eyes. The music was playing softly. Richter's head was bent, his face very close to his own. What finely modelled lips he had. How noble the shape of his head. How strong yet gentle his hands.

Everything flowed then in a warm stream of compulsion and inevitability. He fell headlong into the pit that had been dug for him: dug by himself, too, and the essential weakness of his nature, as much as by the scheming, perverted selfishness of the man who dominated him.

Connie Gates was loath to leave the mess. Her duties ended after dinner, but she chose to stay and help the barman: carrying drinks into the ante room gave her an excuse to cast an eye over the youngsters who were the source of her never-ceasing anxiety.

It was only ten-o'clock, but the place was half-empty already. There was a subdued air over the whole station and everyone was talking in low voices tonight.

Squadron Leader Maxwell had come in with his boys for a quick drink and then, with Flight Lieutenant Poynter, left early. Bernie Harmon had not come to the mess at all: she could picture him jumping on to his bike as soon as the squadron was told to stand down, and pedalling furiously home to his dewy Sarah.

Blakeney-Smith had seated himself among a group: Peter Knight, Six-gun Massey, Jumper Lee and – her heart skipped a beat – Nigel Cunningham and Roddy Webb. They were all sober and quiet. Connie was surprised that Knight hadn't gone to see that pretty girl of his; but this was one of those times when none of the squadron, except those with wives to go to, was willing to desert the others. She understood that, as she understood so many other moods and motives of these young men.

Cunningham gripped a tankard until his knuckles shewed white. He was thinking about the bad moment when he had wavered between trying to forced-land or baling out The long seconds of hesitation came back to him clearly. Memories of battle were compounded of intimate details peculiar to each man's own trade. For fighter pilots the background noise of battle was the whistling of their gun ports after they had blasted the sealing canvas strips away with the first burst of gunfire. That whistle was ever present and they took it for granted, yet when they thought about a sortie afterwards it was something they remembered. The smell of cordite was another, from their own guns and the explosion of enemy shells. And the noise of a bullet through the cockpit: a vicious, short-lived whine; or the slam of a cannon shell through a wing. And the leaping and bucking of a Hurricane or a Spitfire when it was hit.

To add to these, Cunningham now had the experience of what it was like to bale out.

It had been unpleasant remembering what he had seen done to other parachutists; what he had done himself.

Added to the accident of the morning, that horrifying episode of the whirling, headless body and the blood spattering from his propeller, and on top of yesterday's horrors when he had seen the parachuting Hurricane pilots shot down, and then his own inhumanity, baling out today had made a burden he could not carry.

He said quietly "I'm going to bed, Roddy."

Webb looked at him, unhappy. "Me too. I've had enough for today."

Connie watched them go to their rooms at the far end of an upper corridor.

"D'you sleep well, Nigel?"

"Sometimes I can't get to sleep for an hour or more after I'm in bed."

"I know what it's like. Same with me. Look…" Webb hesitated and touched his friend's shoulder diffidently. "If you can't sleep, come to my room and we'll keep each other company…"

Cunningham turned his head and looked at him frankly, "Thanks, Roddy. I'll… I'll remember…"

He went to his room and sat on the edge of his bed, in the dark. He was trembling.

His whole upbringing had been designed to give him self-reliance, yet he desperately felt the need for someone to lean on. He was used to fending for himself: he had been sent to boarding school when he was seven, and ceased depending on his parents.

He was not ignorant of life. Public schools are not the breeding grounds of perversion that their detractors pretend, but neither do they foster innocence.

Sitting in the dark with his body aching and his mind confused, he longed for the physical contact with his friend which had tacitly been offered to him. If only he could share a bed with someone who was suffering the same mental and physical discomforts as himself, perhaps sleep would come easily. That was all either of them wanted: peace of mind and sound sleep; rest for brain and body.

There was no other way. He had tried getting drunk and that had not worked.

He switched on the bedside light and began to undress.

The sheets were cool and soothing but he knew they could not bring him sleep.

For twenty minutes he lay, the light out, his arms folded under his head, moving restlessly. The door opened and he sat up hurriedly. There was a thin streak of light from the corridor before the door closed and darkened the room once more. His voice was uncertain and more than a little afraid: "Roddy?" He heard the key turn and asked again "Is that you, Roddy?"

"Ssh."

"Who is it?"

"It's all right. Lie down."

"Corporal Gates!"

"*Connie*, m'dear."

"You can't... What are you doing here?"

The answer was a low, provocative laugh and he heard the rustle of falling garments. Then there was the scent of powdered flesh and Connie's warm body was beside him, her fingers on his buttons and pyjama cord.

She kissed him. "Lie still... No, not that way... Here... Now come here... Turn this way a little m'dear..." And presently, with a giggle. "Haven't you ever been with a girl before, Nigel? No? I can tell you haven't, m'darling..." And later: "That's better..." and her deep contented sigh.

He called out uncontrollably in his ecstasy, and when he had made love to her the first time he subsided shuddering in her arms, but she would not let him rest: her kisses, her skilled and gentle hands, soon set him alight again and this time it was longer and slower and even more like being struck by lightning. And then it was all over and he was asleep, breathing deeply and evenly. Connie kissed his cheek and left him.

Robby Webb had lain awake for an hour, his mind ranging far and wide in search of some tranquil thoughts which would bring sleep to him. He shifted from side to side, pummelled his pillow, threw off the blanket, then pulled it up to his chin. Sleep would not come.

God! Why didn't Nigel understand how badly he needed his companionship, his physical reassurance? If they could comfort one another instead of being alone, tomorrow would lose some of its menace. He remembered how, when he was ten and his brother eight, and their mother died, they had lain in each other's arms all night until their weeping ceased and the loneliness went. He needed the same comfort now and wanted to give it in return. Someone to share with, who would ease the fear from his mind.

He heard the door creak and pushed himself on to one elbow in time to see a sliver of light before the door shut.

Hope, relief and joy were in his voice: "Nigel?"

The sound of bare feet on the linoleum and the bedside rug. The smell of fresh soap… perfume… glowing flesh.

Startled, he exclaimed more loudly "Nigel?"

"Don't be frightened, Roddy m'dear…" That rich west country burr!

Incredulous: "Corporal…?"

"*Connie*, m'darling. Move over, Roddy." A lascivious giggle. "My! You are a big chap, and no mistake. I'm glad to say!"

He took her eagerly in his arms. It was more than a year since he had been in bed with a girl: at a seaside tennis tournament, and he had been trying to see her again ever since. Now Connie administered her never-failing panacea for what ailed over-tense young pilots.

In fairness, she tried not to make comparisons between her lovers; but tonight there was one fact she could assert: she had satisfied herself twice as much as she had pleasured either of them.

Tuttle, still waiting for leave and the opportunity to misrepresent himself as a fighter pilot, had not yet succeeded with the virgin W.A.A.F. from No. 1 O.M.Q.

On most evenings he took her out, either to a village pub or the camp cinema. At station dances he partnered her untiringly. She rewarded him with much kissing and embracing, but smartly slapped his hand away when he ventured under her clothes. He would have abandoned her for a more certainly acquiescent prey, but was allured by her virginity and piqued by her resistance.

On his way to dinnertime duty in the Officers' Mess, he called at the W.A.A.F. officers' quarters to say a few cheerful words to the two batwomen. He found his young virgin in tears.

"Never mind, love, I'll 'urry back a'ter dinner an' we'll go down the boozer an' 'ave a nice drink; that'll make you feel better."

His words were kindly meant and he had no baser motive than usual, but her ardour was roused by the instinct which seeks to compensate for death by urging humanity to procreate: helped by alcohol and gratitude for Tuttle's sympathy.

So she had parted with the virtue which her mother had enjoined her to preserve intact, and neither she nor her seducer enjoyed the occasion very much.

Henceforth, carnality would always be associated in her mind with the dank odour of an air raid shelter, the reek of metal polish and aircraftmen's serge; and the hardness of a gas mask haversack under her buttocks to raise them conveniently off the unresilient concrete floor, which would not give to Tuttle's awkward knees.

When all was accomplished, and Tuttle feeling none of the elation he usually experienced, she whispered timidly, "Do you really love me, Norm? You do, Norm, don't you?"

He assured her briskly that he did. After all, he told himself, if she's good enough ter screw she's good enough ter marry; if I 'as ter. With ordinary luck, he wouldn't have to; he had taken the customary precautions.

Even had he known that her surrender was a side effect of the German air raids, he might still have thought the damage done and lives lost at East Malford were worth it.

Her bed was vast and spongy. So, reflected Greiner, was Madame Prudhomme.

With her great arms enfolding him, her billiards-table legs wrapped about his matchstick ones, her massive breasts flattened against his bony chest, he was like a whitebait in the embrace of an octopus.

It had been an anti-climactic capitulation and she still would not, coyly, let him use her Christian name or call him other than "Herr Greiner". She, he knew, was named Blanche; but evidently some lingering sense of impropriety still forced her to delude herself that this was not happening. First-names would come in time, he told himself with drowsy contentment.

They had been sitting in the kitchen when they heard the footfalls of Hafner and Ihlefeld returning early from the mess. The heavy front door slammed. Greiner put down his newspaper, gave Madame Prudhomme a wry smile, and went off to see what he could do for his officer. Ihlefeld's batman was not received in the widow's living quarters and came in, grumbling, from the barn.

Hafner was dejected and sleepy. He let his servant help him off with his boots and fold away his clothes, then dismissed him.

Greiner returned to the kitchen, knocking respectfully before entering, to find a glass of calvados and a slice of cold apple pie and cream awaiting him.

He looked his astonishment.

With a self-conscious smirk, Madame Prudhomme said casually: "I felt like a snack. I thought you might join me."

She dropped her eyes, which still had the long lashes of a girl, and Greiner's heart began to flutter. "*Merci bien, Madame. Vous êtes bien aimable… Bon appétit… et santé.*"

"*Bon appétit, Herr Greiner. A la vôtre.* You are a kind man, Herr Greiner: you share all the tribulations of your young officer, and you care for him like a good uncle."

Her speech was suspiciously thick and he guessed that she had profited by his absence to visit the calvados bottle more often than the modest tot she now had before her would suggest.

"I do my duty, dear lady. They are young and they suffer much: at any moment they may lose everything; if not their lives, at least their limbs, their sight… or their sanity. I do what I can to make life easier for them; while they still have it."

"You are a good man, and I do not think you are sufficiently appreciated." She looked him in the face, boldly. "By anyone."

He laughed away her praise. "Come now, how can you say that when you are being so flattering?"

"It is not flattery, Herr Greiner. It is the truth. And you deserve a share of the concern you shew for others. You have been very kind to me, too…"

She looked at him directly once more, then lowered her lashes and they ate in silence.

Abruptly, she pushed back her chair, rose and said quietly: "I shall not lock my door," Then with meaning, "You are a slow drinker."

Ten minutes later he was in her bed and she was devouring him. At the moment of fulfilment she burst into tears and he found himself calming her and crooning to her as though she were a child who had been punished. In a strange, uninvolved way they shewed each other an infinity of tenderness and when, later, he lay wrapped by her abundant softness, he felt marvellously at peace.

In the small hours of the morning he was awakened by a shot and leaped away from her as though a whip had been laid across his bare shoulders. Scrambling into shirt, trousers and boots, he ran upstairs and along the passage outside the officers' rooms.

Hafner and Ihlefeld were there before him. The other officers crowded behind them.

Hafner turned a bloodless face and said harshly, "Go back to bed. All of you. At once!" Then as they lingered, sleepy and dumbfounded, he shouted, "Go on, get out. Greiner, come here."

Greiner pressed himself against the wall to let the others pass, then went up behind Hafner and Ihlefeld who blocked the door. "Fetch the Medical Officer," Hafner ordered, his voice shaking. "And the Adjutant."

Greiner stole a glance into Keiling's room: the boy lay across his bed with a Luger dangling from his hand and the top of his head blown off.

Greiner was familiar with the phrase "to die of shame"; he did not know that he was looking at a tragic expression of it.

THE DAY DAWNED CLOUDY.

Knight, waking to Tuttle's usual heavy-handed prod, sat bolt upright with a start and blinked at his watch.

"Christ! Tuttle, what the hell's the matter with you? It's eight-o'clock. We're on dawn readiness…"

"It's all roight, sir. Dawn readiness is cancelled…"

Knight sprang out of bed and pulled back the curtains; took one brief look at the sky, grumbled and got hurriedly back into bed. "Lousy weather."

"That's roight, sir. Ops phoned through and said everyone's stood down till ten-ow-clock."

Breakfast that morning was less silent than usual. Like Bomber and Coastal Command crews, who celebrated cancellation of night operations with a spontaneous party, the pilots of the East Malford Wing rejoiced at the release from immediate readiness and shewed it by unwonted chatter.

Webb came into the dining-room a few minutes after Cunningham and asked chirpily "Sleep well, Nigel?"

Cunningham, wondering how much the other had heard through the wall which divided their bedrooms, smiled slyly. "Best night's sleep I've had since I got here."

Webb rubbed his hands. "Me too."

Each of them felt smugly amused by his private thoughts, thinking he had scored off the other.

Connie came by briskly, bearing two plates of bacon and egg. Both tried to catch her eye; with no success.

Lotnikski was disgruntled. Non-flying weather meant loss of German-killing time. He hurried through his breakfast and went to the ante room, to stand at one of the big windows and stare at the clouds while he smoked furiously. These damn English didn't allow smoking in the dining-room, and he couldn't last more than fifteen minutes in comfort without a cigarette. He and Dunal had always complained about it. Dunal. He frowned at his thoughts. Not a bad type for a Frenchman. Pity he had to go like that. Very unsatisfactory. He hoped it never happened to him. When he went, he wanted it to be in the excitement of a biasing fight, with his bullets hammering into some Boche. He stubbed out his cigarette and set out for dispersals. It was only nine-o'clock, but he felt less uneasy near his Hurricane than hanging about in the mess.

Blakeney-Smith was lolling contentedly in an armchair, reading *The Times*. As far as he was concerned, they could scrub flying for the rest of the day. Every extra few hours of unthreatened living were worth anything; let the Jerries come over, let them bomb wherever they wanted to: just leave him in peace. He had had more than enough of this bloody war. On the surface he was still the hearty extrovert. He deplored the bad weather as convincingly as Lottie; except that the Pole said very little and it was his eyes which betrayed his frustration, the frequent tugging at his collar which announced his anxiety. With his corn-coloured hair, pale grey eyes and pasty complexion, Lotnikski looked permanently worn out. Blakeney-Smith prided himself that his own florid cheeks and luxuriant black moustache gave him an air of constant good health. If he believed in that sort of thing any longer, he would willingly say ten Hail Marys for continuing bad weather. Instead, he lit a Turkish cigarette and hid behind the newspaper.

Knight went to the telephone after breakfast, to call Anne.

"I missed you last evening," he told her.

"I missed you too, darling. Did you have a good night's rest?"

"Wizard. Didn't have to get up early, either."

"The weather? I hope it stays like this all day, for you." "We'll never win the war if we can't fly."

"Perhaps they'll just give up. After all, they can't fly either." There was a catch in her voice underneath the flippancy.

"I expect we'll be released early, anyway."

"When shall I see you?"

"Early as possible. And, Anne..."

"Yes, Peter?"

"I love you."

"I love you, too."

It was not an exchange of passionate avowals which would go down in history, but it left them both glowing with happiness.

It was as though the sky wept for Manfred Keiling.

So thought Hafner when he woke that morning and stared out of his window. He was grateful for the bonus of sleep the foul weather had granted him. The sight, the shock, of a comrade's suicide, had brought nightmares in its train. He had woken twice, sweating and shaking, before at last he slept undisturbed.

And now his first waking thought was of that Violent death he was well used to by now, but self-destruction was something else: and when the manner of it was so repellent it filled the onlooker with distaste rather than sympathy. Why the hell should Keiling add to the strain of their daily lives by this crudity, this confession of weakness? By what right did he take his own life in this cowardly and messy way, when he could have left it to the British to do the job for him; with honour?

Richter went about his duties that day like an automaton. He had to go to Gruppe Headquarters and report Keiling's suicide. It was a humiliation to the Staffel. Everyone would suppose that the boy had done it because he could not face battle again. Only he knew the truth, and he knew that he lacked the courage to tell it Keiling's name would bear the stigma of cowardice in the face of the enemy for all time, for his suicide would be regarded as the equivalent. His comrades would believe that he had shot himself because he hadn't the courage to fight again.

Richter had sat up all night with the brandy bottle, but found no solace; nor the courage to confess.

But Keiling's parents would never know that their son had killed himself. For them, he would compose a letter of condolence which would conceal the truth. As for the truth behind the truth, that was something to torture him for the rest of his days.

The greyness of the dripping sky matched the gloom pervading the Staffel. The general air of anger and resentment intensified Hafner's preoccupation with vengeance personified. He approached the Intelligence Officer. "Let me have another look at the R.A.F. Order of Battle. I want to verify something."

The I.O., flattered by this interest in detail which the pilots usually treated with frivolity, handed him the file giving the disposition of the R.A.F. fighter squadrons, which had been identified by their marking letters and radio transmissions.

"So 172 Squadron is still at East Malford," Hafner said. "I hope the swines aren't moved after our visit yesterday."

"Small chance, of that," the I.O. replied. "The British have no replacements. Why are you so interested?"

"Every man needs to fix his mind on one particular objective; it provides a reason for survival: to let oneself be killed without achieving it would be intolerable."

The older man tried to soothe him. "You don't need any special objective to keep you alive, Erich. Just look after yourself, don't burden yourself with any other worries."

"The 172 Squadron pilot who flies with the letter "E" on his Hurricane. I'm going to kill him."

"That's foolishness. While you're looking for him you'll let all the others slip by. Or get jumped yourself."

"No, I won't. All the time I'm on the lookout for him."

"If it'll make you feel any better, here's a note on 172 Squadron which has just come in: H.Q. have sent out new lists of the names of all pilots in the R.A.F.'s front line squadrons. And some photographs also."

"I'm glad you ferrets are some use. Let's see what you've got." Hafner took the dossier which the I.O. handed him and ran his finger down a page.

"I wonder what my man's name is… Maxwell… Lee… Poynter… Harmon… Blakeney-Smith… Massey… Knight… *Knight!*" He looked up excitedly. "Have you got photographs of any of these?"

"There's one at the back of the folder."

Hafner turned the papers over until he came to an enlargement of a group of 172's pilots standing in front of a Hurricane, taken a few days before the outbreak of war. He scanned the faces, his heart beating fast, then exclaimed "There he is!" He verified his recognition by quick reference to the names printed under the picture. "My God, this makes him so much more… more… destructible. Thank you, Ferret: you've given me exactly what I wanted."

That afternoon took Hafner a step nearer to the end of his road.

At three-o'clock the clouds broke and the sun shone through. Within thirty minutes a raid was mounted against Southern England, with Richter's Staffel among the escort.

They were in action even before they crossed the coast, and with an exultant shout Hafner saw that their interceptors came from 172.

As always happened, the formations were split up and scattered widely. Hafner found himself and his Schwarm in battle with two Hurricanes. He saw an Me. 109 go down in flames and another turn away with a Hurricane in pursuit. Then he and the other surviving 109s gave themselves completely to the task of shooting down the second Hurricane.

It was an untidy dogfight, but all the time the two Germans were forcing their enemy southward. They had almost reached the French coast when coolant began to pour from Hafner's machine and, simultaneously, smoke billowed from the Hurricane's engine.

The two fighters side by side, slammed down to a crash landing barely inside the Staffel's own aerodrome. Both pilots were out of their cockpits in a trice and running from their aircraft before the fuel tanks exploded.

Ten minutes later Hafner was chatting to the prisoner, a very young and inexperienced sergeant whose reaction to this narrow escape from death was typical talkativeness. With adrenalin super-charging his system, and additionally stimulated by a liberal tot of cognac, he was as excited as though he were at a party instead of being a captive of the enemy.

"And how," asked Hafner casually, "is Flight Lieutenant Lee?" He glanced at the I.O.

"Jumper Lee?" The incautious sergeant repeated. "He's fine."
"I always recognise him by his aircraft." Hafner gave a friendly laugh. "I regard him as an old friend."

"You do? How d'you mean you recognise him by his aircraft?"

"With the little dog chewing the bone, and the letter "E"…"

"Oh! That's not Lee, it's Peter Knight. He's got a small dog, you know: sort of terrier. Called Moonshine…"

The Intelligence Officer was gratefully making notes. Nothing shook newly captured prisoners more than the revelation that the enemy was familiar with these intimate details of squadron life. Unwittingly, the raw sergeant had given away a lot. Lee's nickname… the name and breed of Knight's dog… the identity letter of his Hurricane. Hafner had been a great help in getting him to chatter.

And Hafner, at last, had created an image of his personal enemy. So it was Peter Knight! He might have known their paths were fated to cross again: their backgrounds had so much in common; and so little.

Later that day he spent a long time gazing at his chosen antagonist's cherry face among his companions. Old memories came, bringing alive the forgotten humiliation and resentment of defeat. So, in the end, this had proved to be a very real personal affair indeed.

Richter sat bowed over his writing table, his head supported on one hand, a pen idle in the other. What more could he say? He was half-drunk, and uncertain whether this made his task easier or harder.

"It is with the deepest regret and sense of personal bereavement that I find it my sad duty to write and inform you of the loss in action today of your son Manfred. No one could have wished a more glorious or gallant end to a short, but brave and already distinguished, career…"

He stared at the lies he had written, his pen quivering in his tight grip. He compressed it harder and it snapped; ink spurted out, defacing the writing, splashing his cuff.

He looked miserably at his ink-stained hand and the ruined letter.

It was no use cursing. He simply had to get this damned letter written tonight. He reached for the cognac bottle and shouted to his orderly to fetch him another pen from somewhere.

THE UNPREDICTABLE LATE AUGUST WEATHER allowed them another twenty-four hours of comparative idleness.

While ground crews laboured to take advantage of this lull and bring Spitfire and Hurricane squadrons up to strength, the pilots sat in their crew rooms, prey to a new kind of nervous tension. On the one hand they welcomed the respite, which gave them the chance to make up for lost sleep by dozing all day in an easy chair. On the other they hated the postponement of the inevitable; they knew that they must go into action again sooner or later, and it was perhaps less wearing on the nerves to plunge into it than merely contemplate it.

Their enemies greeted the clouds and rain with the same mixed feelings. Confident though they still were, as September came, that they would conquer England before many more days passed, they were as weary and fear-ridden as its defenders.

II JG 97's No. 1 Staffel had buried Keiling with military honours in a steady drizzle. Not one of the officers attended the ceremony with any feeling of sympathy. Even Richter felt out-raged by the sham; he had reconciled himself to the boy's suicide and exonerated himself from blame for it. Weak material of that kind was bound to destroy itself, and he even persuaded himself that he had done well to precipitate the deed. A gutless fighter pilot was a danger to his comrades. If Keiling had survived he would surely have deserted his leader at some crucial moment in battle. His death certainly meant life to one, or more, of his fellows. Half-baked philosophy and undiluted cognac were power-ful agents of self-delusion.

Only Hafner, of them all, tried to dredge up some emotion from the darkness of his benumbed soul. Somewhere in him there still lurked a few frayed fragments of some kind of faith in God. The rest were all unbelievers, worshipping only the Führer and the swastika, if they worshipped anything Hafner stood at the graveside fingering the holy medal his mother had given him all those years ago in Rome, when he was a child. Looking into the black pit into which Keiling had disappeared for ever, he felt queasy. A spasm of fear forced him to close his eyes, shutting out the sight of that hideous gash in the cemetery turf. He pressed the little medallion hard between his thumb and finger and tried to pray; for himself rather than for Keiling.

The rest of the day limped as leadenly as the colour of the low-ering sky. In their recreation tent at the airfield the pilots played the gramophone, gambled, smoked and fretted for something to do.

Hafner left a card game to sit by himself and brood. Chewing on his knuckles, he set himself to recall everything he could about Peter Knight They had quickly become friends. But were they ever really friends? Could they share a true friendship, when they were fundamentally so opposed? It must have been a false emotion. He had gone to England surfeited with physical adventures with com-plaisant Nazi-bred girls; a sensuality which had first been satisfied at the age of fifteen, and countless times since. He had sensed that the English boy was completely inexperienced, living the almost monastic life which an expensive British education enforced. He had admired him and his dedication to everything that seemed to Hafner to be worthily masculine. Here was true virility: the ca-pacity for self-denial, the hardships of severe athletic training, the spartan life away from home comforts and parental sympathy or protection, the discipline.

Looking back now he acknowledged that, in those distant days, Knight had been a hero to him. What he had mistaken for friendship was only admiration. Well, he no longer admired him. He was going to kill him. And in doing so he was conferring an honour on him; seeking him out for single-handed mortal combat. He wished he could let him know what lay in store; he would like him to be conscious of the event, when the time came. As it was, Knight would die never knowing that his former friend had shewn him such chivalry.

The gramophone in the pilots' crew room played "These Foolish Things" and two or three voices parodied the words obscenely to the amusement of the listeners. In the airmen's rest hut, a wireless set blared "We'll Meet Again", accompanied by the troops' chorus of more or less harmonious, and stickily sentimental, crooning.

Knight felt relaxed and well rested. His mind was so full of Anne that little room was left for introspection. It was his nature to be cheerful rather than morose. This sudden respite had at once restored him to his habitual blithe, mildly ironical detachment. And now that he was in love, his mind was happily occupied. If he kept looking at his watch it was not from anxiety lest the weather improved before it was time to stand down, but because he was eager to go to Anne.

An aviation magazine lay open on his knees. He took a photograph from his pocket, laid it on the page, and admired it. She was the prettiest girl friend he had ever had. He'd love to see her in a bathing costume. He wanted so much to go to bed with her; but he knew he wouldn't. He could be sure of her passion: there was no doubt about that from the way she petted with him. He was too much a product of his environment even to consider whether Anne would rather wait until they were married. With the faulty understanding of women which was so typical of young men of his class and time, he perpetuated a false notion of "nice" girls and "easy" ones. He would have been perturbed to know that Anne, though thoroughly "nice", would be as "easy" with him as any of the mess's camp followers, because she was in love with him. His self-confidence, though modest enough, gave him a superior view of lesser sportsmen and flyers which led to a certain cynicism.

But he had not yet learned to be cynical about girls.

Their short-lived reprieve ended at dawn the next morning. The East Malford squadrons had hardly arrived at their dispersal areas when the Operations Room telephone rang in 172's crew room.

A few sneak raiders were about, probably on weather reconnaissance rather than bombing. A pair of Hurricanes was ordered off: Sqdn. Ldr. Maxwell sent Blakeney-Smith and Webb.

Half an hour later Webb returned alone. "I don't know what happened. We didn't see anything, then Simon said he'd spotted a bogey ten thousand feet above and told me to stay on the patrol line while he went up to have a look at it. A couple of minutes later he gave "Tallyho", but I couldn't see him. Then the controller told me to pancake…"

Blakeney-Smith came back twenty minutes later, with a story about an interception… a Me. 110, which had bolted for France… a fight over the Channel… the Messerschmitt shot down into the sea…

Harmon, disgustedly, commented: "If seagulls could climb to twenty-five thousand, I'd put that down as one seagull destroyed, Spy."

The first squadron scramble came at what, in a civilised existence, would have been breakfast time. The enemy, as though venting their pent-up wrath at two days of frustration, came in strength and fought with outstanding ferocity. In a crazed whirligig of Spitfires, Hurricanes, Heinkels and Messerschmitts, Webb was heard to call out that he was baling out. Soon after the rest of them got back to base they learned that he had been picked up by the Army, with an arm severed and both legs riddled by bullets.

Cunningham, shaking and angry, murmured "There goes a future Davis Cup player." Lost international tennis glory belonged to an almost forgotten era, but nobody thought it bathetic.

After forty-eight hours' taking it easy, people were restless. They didn't have to restrain themselves for long. They were sent off again in mid-morning; and this time it was one of the best of them who didn't come back. Someone who had been an inspiration and a sheet anchor to many. Losses among the least experienced members of the squadron were expected and did small damage to morale, but when a veteran of Jumper Lee's standing was shot down and lost it struck severely at the confidence of the rest.

It was hard to believe that his ebullient laughter and offhand authoritativeness would no longer be heard. Nobody had seen him go down. He had made no final call on the radio. If he had crashed on land, word would come soon. If he had fallen into the sea, either their own or the enemy rescue boats would probably pick him up. If the latter, they might have to wait weeks for the news.

Maxwell and his pilots watched the sky and listened, but the last Hurricane had landed and they had to resign themselves to Jumper's fate. The Squadron Commander beckoned Knight to his side. "I want you to take over "A" Flight, Pete."

"All right, sir; until Jumper gets back."

Connie brought their lunch out and there was a stir of interest. Anything to take their minds off Webb, who had established his popularity, and Jumper for whom they all had such affection.

The other two squadrons had had a bad time that morning. Jerry was back with a vengeance.

And, by God! Here he came again.

Knight flew for the rest of that day with a strange sensation of light headedness. He had been angry many times, frightened many times, determined and aggressive many times; but this feeling of emptiness in his stomach combined with dizziness of the head was new. It had nothing to do with hunger, for he had eaten four thick beef sandwiches at lunch time. He had slept well for three successive nights, so his brain should be clear and rested, yet he felt as though he were permanently on the verge of greying out.

It was a subconscious anticipation of the mental and physical exhaustion which, itself, produced these symptoms. Subliminally, he was aware that, by the end of the day, he would be feeling as worn out and ragged as he had been before the bad weather gave him a rest So he suffered from a mild manic depression. He was faced once again with the demands of six or eight scrambles every day, daily casualties and all the misery of death and injury among his friends.

Webb… Jumper… Wilkins… some whom he had known only for a short time but who were as closely knit to him as old friends. Blakeney-Smith still survived. He had been flying in the same section as Webb when the boy was shot down. He was Jumper's Number Two when Jumper bought it. And there was that strange affair this morning of his claim for an unconfirmed victory after an alleged chase across the Channel. All this weighed on Knight's mind.

Scramble came after scramble, and each time they made contact with the enemy. Sometimes the fight was over in a few minutes and the Germans turned back to prepare for yet another raid. Sometimes a sortie lasted for an hour and someone didn't come back to East Malford. Knight's resentment and his bitterness against this incessant death and destruction smouldered all through the day.

The squadron was on its fifth scramble. Knight, with thoughts of Jumper Lee and Roddy Webb forcing their way through his concentration, knew how tired and nervy he must have become.

The enemy was everywhere. Where did the sods all come from? One minute there wasn't one in sight, and the next they were thick enough to walk on.

The R/T was crowded with warning cries and yells of triumph.

"I got another…"

"Behind you, Green Two…"

"Break right, Six-gun, break right…"

And while this accompaniment dinned in his ears his eyes were darting from side to side, to his mirror, to his reflector sight. His hands and feet were never still as he made constant small adjustments to ailerons, elevators and rudder. His thumb jabbed at his gun button.

Swarms… myriads… hordes… fleets… Heinkels… Dorniers… screaming Stukas… 109s… 110s… Hurris… Spits… collision… ack-ack… some clot in a Spit shooting up a Hurricane… a 109 flying right into the cone of fire from a clutch of 110s.

Thoughts, sensations, rational, coherent, jumbled… decisions… noise… his own guns, the enemy's, his friends'… explosion of bomb load or petrol tank… flashing succession of visual impressions, smoke, flames, debris, parachutes…

Suddenly Massey's voice, instantly recognisable despite the microphone distortion. "Someone help, for Chrissakes…"

A needle through his spine, his brain tingling. "Where are you, Six-gun?"

"Over Ashford… Angels twenty-two… Three 109s…"

"Coming."

An almost vertical climb, and there they were; five thousand feet above. A frantically weaving Hurricane, three Messerschmitts darting and swooping. He shoved the throttle through the gate, his aircraft trembled and the engine shrieked. His eyes stared fixedly at the dogfight overhead.

He looked beyond it and saw a glitter of reflected sunlight He was in luck: one of the boys was up there, at angels thirty, and he'd whip down on the 109s any second now. But he was just circling lazily... Must be another 109, giving top cover... looking out for someone like him going to Massey's help.

One of the three on Massey's tail had seen him and broken off. Here he came. Flames... din of bullets striking his Hurricane... his thumb pressed hard down... his own stinking cordite filling the cockpit... a burst of crimson and orange, wrapped in grey-black... The Me. 109 tumbled past, Knight's shooting more accurate than the German's. That left only two to dispose of. And the one sitting up there, watching.

And then another clap of thunder... more smoke and flames in a hideous firework display... fatal pyrotechnics twenty-two thousand feet above the earth. Two 109s still, but no Hurricane. Good-bye Six-gun... you poor old bugger... No more "Catch!" No more lazy drawl and endless good natured leg-pulling, and getting drunk together. But only one surviving 109, after all. Six-gun must have got the other with his last burst: it was going down steeply in flames,... over on its back... no pilot baling out. That would have pleased Six-gun. Now for the last of the bastards. And the other one, the one up there at thirty thousand feet, watching it all.

Hafner, seeing him come, turning cautiously to put the sun behind himself, preparing for one swift attack that would be the end of this Englishman, caught sight, for the first time, of his identifying letters: YZ-E! *Gott sei dank*, he had got his chance after all.

But be careful: there was that other Hurricane five thousand feet above, always watching. It had watched the fight which had just ended. Why hadn't it joined in? Perhaps this was what it was waiting for: one Messerschmitt and two Hurricanes, and itself with a height advantage.

He didn't care. He wasn't afraid. He was ready for his enemy. For Knight. For single combat to the death: not his, but Knight's.

Knight, eyes on the nearer Messerschmitt, turned to look, as he thought, at its fellow which was keeping well out of the fight. Then, as the latter banked, he saw the outline of a Hurricane's wings. A sledge hammer hit him in the stomach, and he knew who must be flying it.

He ignored the German. He fastened on his true enemy, the real destroyer of Six-gun Massey; and God knew how many others: Webb... Jumper... he could go on remembering the names of those who had flown with Blakeney-Smith, put their trust in him, and been deserted.

Hafner drew off a little way, climbing warily, sun behind him now, slowly gaining height; but never taking his eyes off Knight, except for an occasional suspicious glance above at the other Hurricane. Wily dogs, these Englishmen. They must be talking to each other on the radio... planning to attack him simultaneously from two sides. But why was the higher Hurricane going away now? He glanced again towards Knight, who was shewing no more inter-est in his Me. 109. While Hafner watched, Knight had increased the distance between them. It looked as though he was going to form up with the other Hurricane. Hafner turned towards them.

Knight saw Blakeney-Smith begin to dive and he guessed what the coward intended: there was cloud ten thousand feet below, and he was going to hide in it. But, to reach it, he had to descend steeply across Knight's flight path. With a shallow dive, Knight could intercept him. He had eased his throttle back, but now he opened it wide again and leaped into pursuit.

Hafner, left far behind by now but still as determined as he was baffled, followed. Surely Knight wasn't going to refuse combat and skulk out of harm's way in that cloud bank? He pushed his throttle right open and the Me. 109 thundered after the enemy.

Four thousand feet to go. Blakeney-Smith was almost in safety. But… suppose it wasn't he? That didn't matter… whoever it was had left Massey to die unaided. Knight sat rigid in his cockpit, braced. The controls were stiff at this high speed. His head was clamped in an invisible vice. Only his thumb on the firing button felt as though it still had any independence of movement.

It was a struggle to move his limbs, but the slightest shift of any of the control surfaces produced violent changes in the aircraft's attitude.

The wind screamed and the engine roared. Knight's heart was racing, the blood pounding in his temples.

He was catching up. The other Hurricane had to fly right across him; it had no other way in which to reach the shelter of the clouds.

Four hundred yards. They were converging. Two hundred. Wait… make sure… not of identity, but of lethal range…

He could see the identification letters now. He had been right.

His thumb pressed hard on the firing button.

Converging lines of tracer leaping away from his wings. Vivid flashes when his bullets struck home. The target shuddered, reared up with its nose pointing skyward, away from the clouds and their promise of sanctuary. Then it fell sideways on to one wingtip. And exploded.

Knight had kept his thumb on the gun button for twenty seconds. He had run out of ammunition after ten. His guns were clattering away harmlessly now, the ammunition trays empty.

Sweat filled his eyes. He shoved his goggles up and dashed a forearm across his face.

Hafner was closing for his kill.

He saw Knight deliberately destroy the other Hurricane and for a moment it was as though he himself had received that blast of gunfire, as though it were his own machine which exploded, he was so astonished and shaken.

God in heaven! That took courage. He shared instinctively in Knight's thoughts and feelings, knew that his terrible moment of revenge must be followed at once by remorse; who was Knight, who was any man, to play the part of God? He sympathised with his enemy, understood his motives, his outrage, the self-discipline that his action had demanded. But now it was his own turn to kill. What Knight had done was his affair and had no bearing on what was going to happen to him now.

Hafner had overtaken the Hurricane, and when Knight altered course a little to adjust his aim, had placed himself between Knight and the clouds. There was no escape for the Englishman. He must fight.

The Messerschmitt bored in and the Hurricane turned defiantly towards it.

Knight knew that he must play for time; edge towards the clouds and hide there as long as his fuel lasted, or dive right through and streak for home at ground level. The German could not possibly stay long: he would not have enough petrol remaining. All he had to do, all he could do, was pretend to take the German on in a dogfight, but make sure never to get in his sights.

They stalked each other. They lunged and parried. They looped, rolled, stall turned and dived. Three times, Hafner knew he had been manoeuvred into a position in which his adversary could fire at him; but nothing happened. So he knew that the Englishman had no ammunition left. He had Knight at his mercy; if he could out-fly him.

He did not, for a second, feel any triumph. He could not kill this man who had ignored him (bravely and with seeming contempt) to do what he believed was more important than engaging the enemy. Knight had deliberately thrown away his power to protect himself. He could not, with honour, take advantage of it.

Angry and disappointed, wishing that they could have ended this conclusively, Hafner winged over into a tight turn southward and set course for home.

Peter Knight came back to East Malford to find the rest of the squadron waiting with such ostentatious unconcern that he knew they had not expected him to return.

He remained in his cockpit, taking a grip on himself. He could find no excuse for his cold blooded and rational act. If he had killed Blakeney-Smith in a fit of wild fury, he might have been able to persuade himself that he did not know what he was doing. But it was not so. All the same he knew that he would never confess what he had done. He knew that, in time, he would have no regrets.

He climbed down and turned, to see Harmon walking towards him from his Hurricane, having apparently landed only a couple of minutes earlier.

Harmon stopped and looked at him expectantly, but didn't ask his usual "How many?"

"They got Six-gun, Bernie." Knight was surprised by the steadiness of his voice.

"I… heard him call. What happened?" Harman's voice gave nothing away: neither sympathy nor regret; nor anything else.

"Three 109s on his tail. I couldn't get there in time. We did get one each, but they chopped him… Two of them attacked together and Six-gun bagged one just before they blew him up…"

"That's a bit of a bugger, isn't it? He was a good type. I wish I could have given a hand…"

Herrick was waiting to de-brief them. Knight was reluctant to make his report. He said: "Go ahead, Bernie. I'm in no hurry."

"As you like, chum." Harmon turned to the I.O.

In a dull voice Knight announced to the rest of the pilots: "They got Six-gun," then he went on towards the C.O., who was standing a few paces apart, with Poynter. They both looked grim. He repeated what he had said.

Maxwell went white around the mouth. Poynter's head tic'ed two or three times and he exclaimed "Bloody hell!" The squadron leader said quietly "They've found Jumper, Peter. Not much left of his aircraft. Knight knew that meant that there was not much left of Lee, either.

Knight nodded and went back to give his story to Herrick. Presently Harmon finished, but stayed standing near the Intelligence Officer. "O.K., Pete," said the latter. "When you're ready."

Knight cast his thoughts back to the moment when the enemy had first been intercepted. His recital went smoothly until he came to tell of Massey's call for help. "He was five thousand feet above me, with three 109s attacking him. I climbed steeply and one of the e/ as broke off to engage me. I fired at it head-on and it caught fire and went down out of control. The other two continued to attack Massey, and before I could get to them they caught him simultaneously from both sides. His aircraft exploded. But he had shot one of them down. It spun out in flames." He hesitated. Looking away from Herrick for a moment, he became conscious that Harmon was still there, eyeing him curiously. He wished the fellow would go away.

Harmon put in, non-commitally, "I can confirm that."

Startled, Knight asked quickly: "Where are you?"

"Ten thousand feet below, a mile behind, and pedalling like stink to join you." A faint, mocking grin flickered momentarily at the comers of Harmon's mouth.

Knight licked his dry lips. "Did you… did you see another… another aircraft about five thousand feet above Six-gun and the three that were attacking him?"

"Yes, I did." Harmon paused, looking hard at Knight. "It was a 109. Obviously doing top cover. I saw you go after him."

Knight felt his face burning. Herrick urged "Go on, Peter. What happened then?"

"I… I decided to go for the other… 109. The one which, as Bernie says, was about five thousand feet above…"

"Why?" asked the I.O.

"To make sure of getting him." There was no hesitation about his reply. He felt cooler now, and this time it was he who stared Harmon down. "I reckoned the nearer one would follow me, anyway, and I'd get a crack at it later. I went through the gate, and the second e/a – the higher one – began a steep dive for cloud cover. He crossed right in front of me and I gave him a long, full deflection burst. He caught fire and blew up. The remaining e/a immediately attacked me. As I had no ammunition left, I was forced into a dummy dogfight until I could dive into cloud or he had to break off through lack of fuel or ammo. In fact, that is what he did: he suddenly broke off the fight and scooted home." He looked at Harmon again. "I thought you said you were trying to join me: what happened to you?"

"My engine had been shot up a bit and I had a sudden drop in revs and oil pressure. I lost speed badly, and had to dive to come out of a stall. I saw you tangle with the last 109, and I saw him break away; so I knew you were O.K. and I got back here as fast as I could."

Knight drawing a deep breath, said "Well, that's about it, then, Spy."

"O.K., Pete. Thanks. Well done."

"I can confirm the second 109," Harmon said off-handedly. "I saw Pete give it a long burst, and it blew up."

"Fine," said Herrick.

The two pilots walked away, towards their aircraft, ostensibly to inspect damage and speak to their ground crews.

Harmon put a hand on Knight's arm. It was a most unusual gesture for him. He loathed physical contact as a rule: they both did, except with nubile girls. His voice was quiet and strangely kind; kindness was not a conspicuous feature of Bernie Harmon's nature. He sounded reassuring, in a way which came oddly from him. "Don't feel bad about it, Pete. I was going to get that bastard myself. Morally, he was as much my kill as yours. We both had the chance, and we both took it You got there first, but my intention was exactly the same as yours." This was a long speech for Harmon. He shook – Knight's shoulder, forcing him to turn and look at him. "If I didn't get him then, I'd have got him the next time, by God! I never trusted the sod from the start. I've watched him. I saw him let Six-gun get it; and Christ knows how many others I didn't see. He deserved what you did. Now forget it, Pete. Forget it."

"I'll have to. It was a bloody awful thing to do…"

"It was a bloody awful thing for that shit to *make* you do. For Christ's sake forget it." Harmon was angry, and, for the first time in Knight's hearing, venomous. The shock of hearing him speak with such contempt and hatred of a dead comrade took away some of Knight's self-loathing.

"I'll forget it, Bernie. I wish to Christ I could forget Six-gun as easily. Or Jumper. Or young Webb… Or…" He fell silent; the sad litany was too long.

Knight woke with a headache. Grumpily he pushed his batman's hand away.

Admonishingly, Tuttle said "Toime ter git oop, sir. It's 'alf past foive."

Moonshine scratched at the door and was admitted.

For a moment all seemed normal, until Knight remembered why he had drunk so heavily the previous evening. But his hand was steady as he took the cup and saucer. And he had suffered no nightmares for killing Simon Blakeney-Smith.

Anne had cried bitterly before he left her, early, and went back to the mess to be with his own kind Seeing her weep for the first time gave him a confused sensation of misery and tenderness. She wept for Jumper… for Six-gun… for Roddy Webb. She had even shed tears for Simon Blakeney-Smith. And he knew that she cried most of all because she Was thinking that it might have been he who was killed or wounded; that it might be his turn today or tomorrow.

Tuttle was taking a long time picking up his shoes and tunic for polishing. Impatiently he said -Go and bring me some aspirins, Tuttle; my head's splitting." Alone again, he lay thinking about Anne and the future.

He knew he could never forget the act to which rage and revenge had driven him. In the years ahead with the fading of emotion, it would be increasingly difficult to rationalise and justify. Anne would not forgive him, if she knew, even though she would want to understand and it would break her heart if harm ever befell him. She was to be his life's companion and their fates were inseparably joined It was a responsibility he had not wanted, but it was her gift and he accepted it gladly. But this was one secret he would never share with her.

The door opened again, to familiar slovenly footsteps.

"Come on, Tuttle, where the hell have you been? Where are those bloody aspirins?"

"Had to borrow some from Mr Blakeney-Smith's room, sir. Y'know, *he's* got… he '*ad* everything. There's a shortage on aspirins, sir, Y'know, there's a war on."

THE END